Brant's Dark Eyes Glittered in the Faint Light.

"Well now, Tina, where's my kiss?"
Tina shivered and he laughed softly, gathering her into his arms. His kiss surprised her at first with its gentleness, then his grip tightened and he drew her nearer with bruising intensity. Desire soared within her, until she came suddenly to her senses. What was she doing here in the moonlight, in the arms of a man who didn't love her?

"No! Get out of my room! And never touch me again!"

"Never, Tina? Very well. When I'm gone you'll have no need to lock your door against me—now or ever!"

Despite her victory, fingers of ice made their way down Tina's spine.

NANCY JOHN

has recently finished serving as Chairman of the British Romantic Novelists' Association. She lives with her husband in Sussex, where they are active conservationists. They also ~~love to~~ ravel, researching background~~~~ that have brought ~~~~

Dear Reader:

Silhouette Romances is an exciting new publishing venture. We will be presenting the very finest writers of contemporary romantic fiction as well as outstanding new talent in this field. It is our hope that our stories, our heroes and our heroines will give you, the reader, all you want from romantic fiction.

Also, *you* play an important part in our future plans for Silhouette Romances. We welcome any suggestions or comments on our books and I invite you to write to us at the address below.

So, enjoy this book and all the wonderful romances from Silhouette. They're for *you!*

Karen Solem
Editor-in-Chief
Silhouette Books
P. O. Box 769
New York, N.Y. 10019

NANCY JOHN
Tormenting Flame

Silhouette *Romance*
Published by Silhouette Books New York

SILHOUETTE BOOKS, a Simon & Schuster Division of
GULF & WESTERN CORPORATION
1230 Avenue of the Americas, New York, N.Y. 10020

SILHOUETTE BOOKS, a Simon & Schuster division of
GULF & WESTERN CORPORATION
1230 Avenue of the Americas, New York, N.Y. 10020

Distributed by Pocket Books

ISBN: 0-671-57017-X

First Silhouette printing July, 1980

10 9 8 7 6 5 4 3 2 1

Printed in the U.S.A.

Chapter One

The narrow lane wound between hedgerows that were bursting into fresh green leaf, and wild flowers starred the verges in a lovely tapestry of colour. A soft breeze came wafting through the window of Tina's little car as it spun merrily on its way carrying the sweet country scent of newmown hay.

Already, though June had scarcely begun, the whole of England had been basking in this glorious weather for more than a fortnight. And the weathermen were unanimous in forecasting that a long hot summer lay ahead. Tina breathed a sigh of blissful contentment, followed instantly by a stab of guilt. She really ought not to feel so excited at the prospect of spending the next three months in this tranquil, leafy corner of Sussex, when coming here had entailed dropping out of the University project led by Charles. The team was spending the whole of the long vacation studying the detrimental effects of industrialisation on the Northern counties during the second quarter of the nineteenth century.

But then, she quickly soothed her conscience, it was Charles himself who had recommended her for this assignment at Hucclecote Hall. He had pointed out what a wonderful subject it offered for her M.A. thesis next year. Surely, if Charles could face such a lengthy separation with equanimity, she could let herself enjoy being here without any feelings of remorse?

Tina flicked a glance at her wristwatch. Only twenty minutes to go before she was due to present herself to the man who had engaged her services. Well, she should be almost at her destination now, as long as the next signpost confirmed that she was still on the right road.

Suddenly and without warning, there was an ominous hissing noise, a bump, and a shudder. Tina ended up with the mini's snub nose slewed right across the roadside verge, its bonnet deep among the feathery spikes of flowering grasses. The engine stalled and there was a sudden hush, as if even the birds had been shocked into silence.

Tina took a deep breath and let off steam in a manner that Charles would have regarded with the deepest disapproval. "Oh, damn and blast, you wretched thing!" she said loudly and crossly.

Her quick repentance, though, was not for Charles but for her beloved 'Red Bomber'—the little scarlet mini that was her friend and companion, her pride and joy. And it wasn't even as if this was the poor little car's own fault, such as an engine breakdown. Hadn't she known perfectly well for at least the past month that the offside front tire was distinctly bald—barely within the legal limit, in fact—and hadn't she postponed replacing it in favour of other, more interesting purchases?

"Sorry sweetie, I didn't mean to be rude," she muttered contritely, giving the steering wheel an affectionate pat. "Am I forgiven?"

To her confusion, Tina became aware of movement beyond the hawthorn hedge, and the upper half of a man appeared. She watched, fascinated, as he unwound his lean length into full view. Towering above her like this he looked a good ten feet tall, though reason told her it must be an illusion. Six foot three, perhaps.

"You've no need to apologise," he informed her in a kindly tone. "I don't in the least object to you swearing if it helps to relieve your feelings."

"But I wasn't apologising to you," Tina choked, her face flushing to match the bright red of her car.

"To whom, then?" One hand held peaked to his forehead, he made a performance of scanning the four points of the compass.

"If you must know," she mumbled, feeling a complete idiot, "it was my car."

"Really?" A look of intrigued amusement crossed his face. It was a face full of character, Tina noted, with a rough cragginess about it, as if its owner was accustomed to spending his time working out of doors in all weathers, exposed to sun and wind and rain. His rich brown hair was tousled, by a hand or the wind. And then, further noting his grubby blue jeans, held up at the waist with a broad, buckled, leather belt, and his checked shirt that was unbuttoned to reveal a deep vee of suntanned chest, lightly matted with hair, she realised that obviously he was a farmworker. He had presumably been engaged in hedging or ditching or whatever when she'd interrupted him.

At least, though, judging from his powerful shoulders and the muscular forearms which emerged from his rolled-up sleeves, he looked amply strong enough to manhandle her baby car back onto the road if need be.

He was saying chattily, with an elusive twang in his voice that didn't sound quite like what she had expected as the local dialect, "Do you make a habit of talking to your vehicle? Tell me, does a mini make a good conversationalist?"

"Very witty!" Tina retorted. "But instead of standing there making fun of me, you might try to help."

"With pleasure!" He vaulted the hedge with an effortless leap, and landed neatly beside her. "What's the trouble? Puncture, I suppose?"

She nodded gloomily. "The tread is worn pretty thin, I'm afraid."

He bent to inspect the offending tire, kicking aside the tangle of buttercups and rose-pink campion.

"You can say that again!" he observed. "I hope the spare's in better shape."

"Worse, if anything," Tina admitted.

He turned a dark frown on her. "If I change the wheel for you now, you'll have to give top priority to getting a new tire. Or rather, two new tires."

"Oh yes, I will," she agreed, with an anxious glance at her wristwatch. "I'd be extremely grateful to you. You see, this has come at a most awkward moment. I'm in a great hurry."

He certainly seemed to know what he was about, she thought with relief, as she watched him fetch the spare wheel and toolkit from the boot, jack up the car and spin off the wheelnuts. Squatting on his haunches as he worked, his shirt was tightly stretched across the muscles of his broad back, and the blue denim of his jeans was strained over his powerful thighs like a second skin.

"Did you hear what I said?" he asked, twisting his head to glance up at her.

"Er no . . . sorry," she apologised, confused and embarrassed.

"Suppose that blow-out had happened on a main road with lots of traffic! You'd have ended up in hospital—or worse! So make damn sure you get two new tires pronto. Right?"

"Right!" she said, chastened. "I promise."

The sternness of his words was swept away by a sudden forgiving grin. His teeth showed in two even lines between lips that shaped an arrogant mouth. His chin was firm and determined . . . aggressive, almost. And his eyes, she saw, were a smoky blue-grey of unfathomable depth.

"You'll learn sense in time, I suppose," he said. "You're just a kid yet."

"I'm twenty-three!" she flared indignantly, her blue eyes flashing.

"Quite the old lady!" he mocked.

With great dexterity he slid the spare wheel into position and tightened the nuts. The jack was lowered in a trice, the replaced wheel and toolkit tossed into the boot, and the lid slammed down.

"All done!" he announced, and gave her a thumbs-up sign.

"That's fantastic!" she exclaimed. "You were so quick. I can't tell you how grateful I am."

"There's a very simple way of expressing your gratitude," he said meaningfully.

"Oh yes. . . ." Tina flushed scarlet once more. Of course, farmworkers weren't all that highly paid and he'd been hoping for a decent tip. Quickly she reached into the car for her shoulderbag. She had unfastened it and was dipping for her wallet when a firm brown hand clasped over hers and drew it away.

"I don't want money!" he rasped angrily.

"But I thought you meant. . . ." Tina gazed up at him, bewildered. "After all, it's only fair, isn't it, when you consider what it would have cost me to call out a tow truck, and I'd have been late for my appointment and everything. . . ."

"The reward I was thinking of," he elucidated, "was that you should give me a kiss."

She stepped back quickly, astonished and dismayed, while he regarded her with frank amusement. Tina couldn't have known how enchanting she looked to male eyes at that moment . . . her silk-fine golden hair teased a little by the breeze, the creamy skin of her small oval face becomingly pink, and her maidenly modesty further betrayed by the rapid rise and fall of her breasts, taut against the thin fabric of her summer dress.

Tina's mind was spinning. The last thing she wanted was a scene, when she was already late for the first meeting with her new employer. Would it be so very dreadful to give her good Samaritan a peck on the cheek? After all, it was really just a bit of fun! No doubt he wanted to boast in the village pub tonight that he'd won a kiss from a pretty girl in exchange for changing the wheel of her car.

She had to admit that, despite the fact that his hands were smothered in black grease (grease from *her* car, she reminded herself), he still looked perfectly wholesome. He was as unlike Charles as chalk from cheese, of course, but really rather attractive in his rough-hewn way. So with a brave smile she stood on tiptoe and administered the kiss he demanded, managing only to reach up to his cleft chin rather than to the cheek she had been aiming for.

"There!" she said shakily. "All square now?"

"I'm afraid not!" he returned. "You're not getting off that lightly."

Tina jumped back hastily, really alarmed now. But the man moved just as quickly and her escape was cut off. The next moment she found herself pinned between him and the door of her car. Even though he kept his black-grimed hands away from her body so as not to soil her primrose dress, the clench of his arms was so strong that she was helpless to move. Furthermore, to her chagrin, she felt herself tingling with a disturbing awareness of the hard masculine body pressed so closely against her. She could feel the warmth of him through the thinness of his cotton shirt, the sheer strength and power of his muscled chest and thighs. Slowly he bent his head and searched for her lips, forcing them to part under his probing tongue. For a long searing moment Tina stood there transfixed, her pulses throbbing, a flame leaping within her, her entire being treacherously responding to him. Then, with an effort, she snapped back to her senses. Her two fists pressing against the solid wall of his chest, she pushed away from him with all her might.

"How dare you!" she cried when at last he let her go.

"Don't try and pretend you didn't like it, Blue Eyes," he jeered.

"Of course I didn't like it," she denied furiously.

"No? It certainly took you long enough to get around to struggling."

"That was only because . . . because you took me by surprise. I never dreamt that you'd behave in such a way."

"Why not?" he demanded. "I'm a man, aren't I?"

"You needn't try to make me believe all men are like you," she retorted, still trembling from the memory of his lean body crushed against hers, the faint tang of him . . . a subtle aroma of aftershave, the musky scent of man.

"Don't make out that I'm some sort of a monster," he laughed, "or I might really start to act like one."

"You keep away from me," she ordered, backing off in alarm.

His look was scathing. "Even now when you're supposed to be so upset, you're standing there with those huge blue eyes and that seductive body of yours giving me a great big come-on."

"I'm not, I'm not!" she cried wretchedly. "I . . . I can't help the way I look."

"Granted! But you make full use of everything you

happen to have—and that amounts to plenty!" His gaze travelled insolently down her full length, taking in every last detail of her female form, then leisurely came up to meet her eyes again. "You'd better get on your way, before I forget myself and lose my self-control."

Uneasily, Tina edged forward and climbed into her car. She started the engine, revved up and shifted into gear before daring to throw him a suitably crushing retort.

"I doubt," she opined, "if you know the meaning of self-control. You're nothing but an uncouth lout."

His dark eyes sparked with danger, and Tina shot away in her car before he could stop her. Reaching the next bend, she got a glimpse of him in the rear-view mirror. He was standing in the centre of the lane, his fists bunched against his hips. He looked terribly angry, she noted with a shudder, and wondered what might have happened if she hadn't beaten such a hasty retreat.

In hardly more than another mile she came to the main entrance gates of Hucclecote Hall. Swinging in between the stone gateposts, each crowned with a carved gryphon, she received a nod from the gatekeeper standing at the door of his lodge. The long driveway led up through a glorious deerpark, with magnificent clumps of standing beeches and an occasional Cedar of Lebanon spreading its dark branches against the intense blueness of the summer sky. Away to her right a crescent-shaped lake shimmered in the sunlight, the stately gliding swans white against the lapis-lazuli of the water. It was a scene of utter peace and tranquility, she thought. The perfect English landscaped garden. Tina knew from the hasty research she'd managed to do so far on Hucclecote Hall that the grounds had been laid out over two hundred years ago by the famous Capability Brown.

Ahead of her was a dip and then a gentle rise crested by a fine yew hedge. Passing this, she caught a teasing glimpse of a little Grecian temple set on a small knoll. Beyond, the park changed to a more formal layout with lawns and shrubs and flowerbeds, and suddenly the house came into view . . . a gracious, time-honoured building of ivy-clad grey stone, with pointed gables and tall twisted chimneys. Its many mullioned windows reflected back the golden rays of the afternoon sun to dazzle and bewitch Tina with its splendour.

Smooth yellow gravel scrunched beneath her tires as she drew the mini to a halt by the great front portico. Should she have come here, she wondered anxiously, or to some other entrance? She would hardly be classified as "Staff," yet what precisely was she? Something of a betwixt and between, she thought with a smothered giggle, like a governess in earlier times—neither a servant nor family.

Getting out of the car, Tina found that her legs were still trembling from that embarrassing encounter on the road a mile back. Confound the wretched man for having this unnerving effect on her just when she needed to be at her best! But in all fairness, she had to acknowledge that but for him she would never have managed to get here in anything like time for her appointment with Brant Wakefield.

An apron of balustraded, stone steps led up to the massive iron-studded front door. It stood wide open, and Tina stepped into a black-and-white tiled lobby and moved forward to the inner, glazed doors. Through these, she could see into the Great Hall, a huge apartment panelled in age-blackened Tudor oak sweeping up to a vaulted ceiling and a pretty minstrels' gallery behind a carved screen.

The wrought-iron bell-pull worked smoothly, and only a few moments passed before a woman appeared from the nether regions in answer to her summons. Opening the door, she looked at Tina enquiringly.

"Good afternoon. I'm Tina Harcourt. I have an appointment with Mr. Wakefield."

The woman's face eased into the faintest of smiles. Aged about fifty, Tina judged, she was wearing a navy cotton dress with only a white neckband to relieve its severity.

"Ah yes, I was told to expect you, Miss Harcourt," she said, the hint of a Scottish brogue behind her voice. "Come inside, if you please. Mr. Wakefield is not at home just at the moment, but I daresay he won't keep you waiting too long."

Really it was too bad, Tina thought bitterly. After going through all that anxiety, and suffering the most dreadful humiliation at the hands of that lustful farmworker, only to be told that the man who had engaged her wasn't here to keep their appointment, after all!

"My luggage?" she murmured to the housekeeper, pulling herself together. "Had I better fetch it from the car?"

"That will be attended to," the woman replied crisply. "I can show you to your room later. You must remain down here just now, to be ready for when Mr. Wakefield arrives."

So, Mr. Brant Wakefield could be late for an appointment of his own making, but clearly he expected lesser mortals to wait upon him subserviently. Tina had half a mind to demand to be shown to her room right now, and keep the man cooling his heels for a while.

As she entered the lofty hall, mellow afternoon sunlight struck through the tall, leaded windows, making mosaic patterns on the marble floor. Stout stone pillars supported the ceiling which was thickly encrusted with an intricate plasterwork design of heraldic emblems. An immensely long refectory table occupied pride of place, surrounded by a set of fine Jacobean chairs whose leather backs were embossed with a coat of arms.

Tina was not left to linger here, though, but shown directly into a much smaller room on the right. By comparison with the lordly entrance chamber it seemed almost cosy and intimate, with beautiful oriental rugs strewn about the floor, and comfortable sofas and armchairs placed casually.

The woman indicated that Tina should take a seat. But she remained standing herself, very stiff and upright, hands clasped together uncompromisingly on her stomach.

"I am Mrs. Moncrieff," she announced. "I was Mr. Sebastian Wakefield's housekeeper for almost twenty years. When the old gentleman died and Mr. Brant Wakefield inherited, he asked me to stay on. He himself only occupies an apartment on the upper floor, but I shall also be supervising the running of the rest of the house when it is opened to the public next spring." She gave Tina a frankly curious glance. "I'm not too clear precisely what it is you've come here to do, Miss Harcourt."

"I've been commissioned to write a history of Hucclecote Hall," Tina told her proudly.

Mrs. Moncrieff pursed her lips, looking doubtful. "You seem very young for anything like that, I'm thinking."

"But it's my special subject, you see," Tina explained eagerly. "I'm reading Social History at Bellchester, and when Mr. Wakefield contacted the University enquiring if they could suggest anyone suitable for the task, my tutor thought of me. . . ." It was unnecessary to explain that she and Dr. Charles Medwyn had a relationship that went far beyond the normal one of

tutor and student . . . a tacit understanding, in fact,
that in the course of time, when she had gained her
M.A. and Charles had succeeded to the Chair of Social
History upon old Professor Walters' retirement, they
would become man and wife. In point of fact, Charles
honestly did consider her the best fitted of his students
to research the matter in question, and Tina was
determined to make a really good job of the book, not
only so as to present it as her thesis, but also to win
Charles' personal approbation.

She gave Mrs. Moncrieff something of a defiant look,
and went on, "I've specialised in the study of the
English landed estates, you see. I already know enough
about Hucclecote Hall to realise it possesses a fascinating history. There's been a house on this very site for
almost six centuries. Just think!"

The housekeeper did not appear to be unduly
impressed. The lifting of her thin shoulders indicated
that for anyone who was accustomed to serve in the
great aristocratic households, such a long pedigree was
the rule rather than the exception. There was the sound
of a door slamming somewhere in the house, and she
looked relieved at the interruption.

"Ah, this will be Mr. Brant," she said, turning to the
door. "I'll just be telling him that you are here, then."

The housekeeper departed and Tina heard her
footsteps ring on the marble floor of the Great Hall.
Then silence. She strolled to the window and gazed out
across the rolling parkland to the tiny private chapel,
nestled in a clump of ancient yew trees, its stone walls
leaning slightly, its tower square and squat. Were
services still held there, she wondered?

Then there were footsteps again, decisive masculine
steps that came briskly to the room where Tina waited.
The door was thrown open and a man strode in, so tall

that he almost had to stoop his head as he passed beneath the lintel.

With a shock of surprise Tina recognised him, and she couldn't suppress the gasp that rose to her lips. Looking quite incongruous here in such gracious surroundings in his grubby jeans and stained checked shirt, it was the man she had met on the road just now. The man whose arrogant lips had been pressed to hers in a kiss that had inflamed her senses and left her trembling. The man she had so enraged by calling him an uncouth lout!

Chapter Two

The man's face darkened with annoyance at the sight of Tina.

"There must be some mistake," he said coldly. "Mrs. Moncrieff informed me that Miss Clementina Harcourt had arrived. What are *you* doing here?"

Tina looked back at him nervously, all her dreams of a lovely tranquil summer crashing to the ground. Could this man, whom she'd taken for no more than a farmworker, really be Brant Wakefield, owner of the vast Hucclecote Hall estate? There was nothing of the aristocratic suavity and polish about him that she had expected, but instead a sort of rough-hewn quality both in his appearance and his manner of speech that didn't at all seem to fit a member of the landed gentry. And those jeans . . . looking even grubbier now, because he seemed to have rubbed off the grease he'd picked up from her car by wiping his hands against his muscled thighs.

"There is no mistake, Mr. Wakefield," she said with all the dignity she could muster—which was precious little at that moment. "I am Clementina Harcourt."

"Don't be absurd, you can't be!" he said brusquely. His brow ridged in a darkly suspicious frown. "Just what's your little game, Blue Eyes?"

"I wish you wouldn't call me that," she objected.

"Why not, when you make the fullest possible use of those alluring optics of yours," he observed sardonically. "Still, if you'll tell me your real name, I'll call you by that."

"I *have* told you my name," she said crossly. "Why won't you believe me?"

"Because," he riposted, with the triumphant air of one whose argument is unanswerable, "Miss Clementina Harcourt is a competent historian who is coming here at my invitation to write a history of my family and this estate."

"And I'm her! Or rather, she," Tina amended feebly, then made yet another attempt to make it sound right. "That's who I am. Clementina Harcourt."

"Nonsense!" He strode across and towered above her in a threatening posture, so that it was all Tina could do to stand her ground. "The lady in question," he went on, "is obviously a great deal older than you, a steady and reliable sort of person who wouldn't dream of driving around on nearly bald tires. Why, the very sound of that name conjures up a picture of staid responsibility."

"Actually, I'm usually known as Tina," she murmured, thereby half admitting a certain logic in his argument.

"Then why," he demanded, eyebrows lowering blackly, "were you recommended to me by the name Clementina?"

"Oh, that was Charles," Tina replied, carelessly off-guard.

"Charles?" he rapped. "Who's he?"

"I . . . I meant to say Dr. Charles Medwyn. He's my tutor at University," she went on hurriedly. "I suppose, seeing that Clementina is my proper name . . . the one that appears on all the official records, he thought it only right to use it."

This explanation was dismissed with an irritated sweep of one of his large hands.

"Tell me," he said, "is it normal practice at Bellchester for the girl students to call their male tutors by their Christian names?"

Tina coloured. "Well no . . . I suppose not. It's just that Dr. Medwyn and I . . . er. . . ."

"Exactly what favours did you bestow upon the man," he enquired bitingly, "for him to recommend you for this important assignment? Merely a few seductive glances from those big blue eyes of yours would hardly have sufficed to persuade a respected University tutor to abandon his integrity."

Tina felt like stamping her foot in sheer rage. Instead, she ground out between clenched teeth, "Your letter to the University authorities was passed on to Dr. Medwyn. It was his considered opinion that I was the most suitable person to suggest, because I happen to be specialising in the study of great landed estates like Hucclecote Hall."

"What vast experience you must have acquired," he remarked cuttingly, "at the venerable age of twenty-three."

Her temper flared and she burst out, "Are you saying that you don't want me to stay and carry out the assignment? Because if so, I'm ready to leave this very minute."

Brant Wakefield did not give an immediate reply, and Tina awaited his response with bated breath. Suppose he was to take her up on this impetuous suggestion? She would have to go crawling back to Charles and confess that she'd let both him and the University down badly, all because of a silly case of injured pride. And what was worse, she'd have to spend these glorious summer weeks of the long vacation traipsing around with him and his party, visiting coal mines and industrial museums and out-of-date, cobwebby factories to further Charles' ardent quest for knowledge. The sort of research waiting to be done here at Hucclecote Hall was so much more to her liking.

Brant Wakefield paced around her in a contemplative circle, and Tina was tinglingly aware of his eyes roaming over her, taking in every last curve of her body and the shapely, lissom limbs; noting her straining breasts and nervously fluttering hands; registering the heightened colour of her peach-soft cheeks and her shy evasion behind her lowered lashes.

"No," he said at last, giving his verdict. "I suggest that you don't run away, Clementina. Now that you're here, you'd better find the guts to face up to the task in hand. But I'm not vulnerable like Dr. Charles Medwyn, so don't expect any special favours from me because you happen to be young and beautiful. I shall regard you simply as someone with a job to do, and I'll expect you to get on with it. I shall do my level best to ignore the fact of your being female," he finished sternly. "That would have been easy, with the woman I had envisioned turning up."

"I only ask to be allowed to get on with things in peace," Tina retorted with a final flash of spirit, though she felt relief flooding through her.

Brant Wakefield nodded carelessly. "Do that! For the rest of today you can just wander around getting the feel of things here. Then tomorrow morning I'll find the time to show you some of the family archives. They're in a pretty chaotic state, it seems to me, though I've not had a chance to more than briefly glance at them in the short time I've been here."

"I'll soon get everything sorted out," she told him confidently.

He was leaving the room, but paused in the doorway as an afterthought struck him.

"I suppose you know where you'll be sleeping, etcetera?"

"No, but Mrs. Moncrieff said she'd show me to my room after I'd seen you," Tina responded.

"Right! Well, that's fine, then!" He went out, leaving her to wonder what she was supposed to do now. Summon the housekeeper by tugging the twisted bellrope which hung beside the carved stone fireplace? Better not, she decided, or it might be thought presumptuous of her.

Fortunately, the problem was solved by Mrs. Moncrieff's appearance at the door. She stood with hands clasped before her in what was clearly a characteristic gesture.

"Well now, I gather that Mr. Brant was as surprised as I was to see just a young lass come to write his book," she observed drily. "Still, he considers that he ought at least to give you a trial to see if you're up to the mark. So come along with me, Miss Harcourt, and I'll show you to your room."

Side by side, they recrossed the Great Hall and went through an archway to a smaller hall from which the grand staircase rose. It was of heavy, solid carved oak, darkened by the passage of the centuries and lovingly polished to a high sheen.

So Brant Wakefield was putting her on trial, was he? Tina thought furiously as they began to climb. Well then, she'd jolly well show him what she was made of! A shiver ran through her at the implication of those words. *What she was made of!* She had a terrifying suspicion that this man could discover her true self only too clearly. For meeting him had awakened in Tina all those shameful emotions she had believed to be so firmly under lock and key. Just now, when Brant Wakefield had faced her with eyes that sparked with scorn, she had felt an electric response to him deep within her being.

Tina gave herself a stern shake. What did such feelings amount to, after all? Mere chemistry! Were they any more important than the stirrings she sometimes felt after a Saturday night dance at the Students' Union, when she was escorted home by some young male student who seized the opportunity to become amorous? There was no denying that such kisses had excited her slightly, bringing her to a sensuous awareness of her feminine body, and the young men's roaming hands and urgently whispered entreaties had frayed her self-control. But Tina had always emerged from the encounters unscathed, confident in the knowledge that true love was the serene emotion she felt for Charles, and he for her.

On the upper landing, the housekeeper led her into what had clearly been divided from the main house to become a separate apartment. It was comfortably furnished in a more modern style than the downstairs. The room she was shown into was well-appointed, the decor a pleasing blend of greens and yellows. Through an inner door that was left ajar, Tina glimpsed a luxurious private bathroom. Her two slightly battered suitcases had already been brought up for her.

"This is very nice!" Tina's comment was meant sincerely, but she also hoped to win a smile from the woman's severe visage. In this she only half succeeded.

"Aye, that it is!" the housekeeper agreed. "Of course, these rooms have only recently been converted for Mr. Brant to live in. Old Mr. Sebastian Wakefield used to occupy the whole of the house, but now that the Hall is to be thrown open to the public Mr. Brant needed some private accommodation."

"He inherited from his uncle just a few months ago, I believe?" Tina queried.

Mrs. Moncrieff inclined her head in acknowledgement. "The direct heir would have been Mr. Sebastian's son, Richard Wakefield. But the poor young man was killed in a road crash just a few weeks before his father's death. Mr. Brant therefore came into the estate as the next in line."

"So, the tragedy of his cousin being killed was Brant Wakefield's good fortune," Tina observed. She felt obscurely pleased at having discovered that it was only a fortuitous stroke of fate that had put this arrogant man in the eminent position he now enjoyed.

"I don't know about that," the housekeeper rebuked her. "Mr. Brant can hardly have been overjoyed to inherit all the worry that goes with a huge place like this. He had his own life out in Australia . . . an enormous sheep station with I don't know how many thousand acres. He's had to leave that in the hands of his managers in order to come over here."

"I wonder why he bothered," Tina remarked scornfully, before she could check herself.

Mrs. Moncrieff had been opening another window, letting in more of the warm afternoon air. Now she turned to face Tina, an affronted expression on her long, thin face.

"I can tell you why he bothered, Miss Harcourt," she returned. "Because he has Wakefield blood in his veins, that's why! He is the only one of the main family left now, and he regards it as his bounden duty to take over the estate and keep the old traditions alive. Unfortunately, with all those heavy death duties to be paid, it's difficult even for someone with Mr. Brant's great wealth. That's why he's planning to raise money in different ways. Not just by opening the Hall to the public, but by reviving all the old crafts that were carried on here in former times. And the book you're supposed to be here to write, that's something else."

Tina felt very contrite. "I'm sorry," she murmured. "Actually, I can understand how Mr. Wakefield feels. Although I don't come from ancient stock myself, I do appreciate how much this country owes to families such as his. Places like Hucclecote Hall are part of our national heritage, and well worth the great effort of keeping them alive."

The housekeeper looked mollified. "You could do with a nice cup of tea, I dinna doubt," she said, very nearly smiling.

"Oh, yes please!"

"Then I'll away and make a pot, whilst you unpack your things, lassie." She hesitated before departing. "I always have a cup myself at about this time of the afternoon, so perhaps you would care to join me in my room?"

"Thank you, yes I would," Tina accepted, feeling that it would help cement their slightly warmer relationship.

"It's the door facing you right at the end of the corridor," Mrs. Moncrieff directed. "Shall we say in ten minutes?"

Tina smiled. "I'll be there."

When the housekeeper had left, she unclipped her cases and started putting her things away in the wardrobe and ample drawer space. Slipping a couple of dresses onto hangers, she paused at the window to admire the view of gently undulating parkland that stretched to the lake, and the soft line of the Downs beyond. A movement just below caught her eye. It was a landrover, and Tina saw that it was being driven by

Brant Wakefield. Another man lolled in the back, similarly dressed in jeans and shirt. Comparing the two of them, she wondered how she could ever have mistaken Brant Wakefield for a farmworker. There were qualities about the man that would never have allowed him to settle for a lowly position in the world . . . authority and superb self-confidence. Plus, Tina suspected, a streak of ruthlessness. He handled the landrover just as he would handle a person, she realised—completely dominating it, subduing the machine utterly to his will.

Mrs. Moncreiff's sitting room was comfortable in a homely sort of way. She invited Tina to take a seat on the well-sprung sofa, and Tina immediately found herself mentioning the man who employed them both.

"Mr. Wakefield doesn't seem to mind getting his own hands dirty," she observed, with a hint of reluctant admiration.

"Aye, he'll tackle anything that needs doing, will Mr. Brant," the housekeeper agreed proudly. "He canna ever rest, he's always finding something to occupy him. There must be a driving force inside him like a tightly-coiled steel spring."

"Is he married?" Tina asked, and was rewarded with a sharp glance.

"Not yet," the older woman replied. "But a wedding will not be long delayed, to my way of thinking."

"He's engaged, you mean?" Tina probed. "To someone he's met since he came to England?"

"Aye!" The response was to both questions. Then, "Well, not precisely engaged. But there is an understanding, you might say. And undoubtedly, from the family point of view it would still be a fine thing—the bringing together of two great estates."

"Still?"

The woman looked slightly discomforted. "She was

going to marry his cousin, you see . . . the previous heir. Then when Mr. Richard was killed and Mr. Brant came to this country to take over, well . . . I suppose it was only natural. . . ."

Tina felt sickened. How dreadfully cold and calculating to switch from one man to another like that! It wasn't a matter of falling in love, but simply of furthering family interests.

"Who is she?" she ventured to ask.

"The Honourable Loretta Boyd-French," the housekeeper supplied.

Tina knit her brows. "Oh, I know . . . she'd be the daughter of Viscount Boyd-French, of Maddehurst Manor?"

Mrs. Moncrieff seemed impressed. "You appear to be well-informed, Miss Harcourt."

It was meant as a compliment, but Tina couldn't summon up a responsive smile. She was gripped by a curious and totally irrational feeling of despair which damped her spirits down to zero. Briskly, she turned to practical matters, but found that even so she hadn't escaped from the disturbing subject of Brant Wakefield.

"Where shall I be having my meals?" she asked.

Mrs. Moncrieff gave her an odd look, and replied, "In the dining salon, Mr. Wakefield said."

"You mean, with him?" Tina queried in astonishment.

"Yes . . . in theory, that is. But I can never rely on the master turning up at mealtimes. When anything needing to be done catches his attention while he's out and about round the home farm, like a broken fence or something . . . well, I have to expect him when I see him."

As it turned out, though, when Tina made her way to the dining room at eight o'clock that evening in

response to the summons of a bell, she found that for
once, at least, Brant Wakefield was on time. In fact, he
was there before her, looking casual but immaculate in
dark slacks and a cream silk shirt worn with a crimson
velvet necktie. As she entered, he put down his glass of
sherry on a marquetry side table, and invited her to
join him in a pre-dinner drink.

"Sweet or dry?" he enquired.

"Oh, dry please!"

The smile he awarded her was full of dancing irony.
"I might have guessed that it wouldn't be sweet for
Miss Clementina Harcourt."

"Are you being sarcastic, Mr. Wakefield?" she
demanded, ready to bristle.

With a shrug he picked up the sherry bottle. "You're
being a shade too touchy, I think."

"I'm sorry," Tina riposted, "that I fall so short of
what you expected of me."

"I'd hardly say that!" His glance was insolent as he
held out the filled glass to her, not just meeting her eyes
challengingly, but taking in the whole of her shapely,
slender body. "I think it would be fair to comment," he
drawled, "that in many vital ways you considerably
surpass my expectations."

Fortunately, the housekeeper came in at that moment bearing a tureen of soup. Brant gave her a
friendly glance.

"It smells like good Scotch broth, Mrs. Moncrieff,"
he complimented her. "A fine start to any meal."

Her expression was fondly gratified, and Tina real-
ised that already in the few months he'd been here
Brant Wakefield had won the woman's devoted loyalty.
Perhaps there was more to this man than she had
thought, she told herself in an attempt to be fair.
Perhaps there was something beyond this overweening

opinion of himself, and the belief that other people should jump to attention whenever he was around.

"You will discover, Miss Harcourt," he went on, "that the food in this house is invariably excellent, thanks to Mrs. Moncrieff's cooking."

"Oh, get along with you, Mr. Wakefield," his housekeeper remarked coyly, as she left the room.

"If you're not careful," he continued to Tina, "you'll find yourself putting on weight, and we can't allow that, can we? It seems to me that you already have precisely the right degree of padding in all the correct places. Doubtless though, you've been told that often enough, eh Blue Eyes?"

This time Tina really did stamp her foot. The effect was somewhat muffled, however, by the thick, springy carpet that covered the entire floor.

"Will you kindly not call me by that absurd name," she flashed. "I'm here to do a serious job, so I'd be obliged if you'd stop all this ridiculous sparring and treat me like a responsible human being."

"I'll be glad to," he observed evenly, "when you've proved that you *are* one."

"And how am I supposed to do that?" she challenged him.

"Quite easily! Just stop using every single ounce of your considerable feminine charm. For example, that dress you're wearing . . . or rather, very nearly wearing. Is that supposed to be serious and responsible?"

Tina felt her whole skin burning with embarrassment. She cursed the inexplicable impulse that had made her decide to wear this particular dress in palest pink voile, elasticized across the low-cut bodice. She had known when she was hesitating in her room that her blue cotton shirtwaist would be better for the occasion. But she had wanted to destroy once and for all the image he had conjured up of a stuffy female suited to the name of Clementina . . . and it appeared she had succeeded only too well!

"It's a very sultry evening," she countered. "Do you expect me to wrap myself up in woollens or something?"

"I don't expect anything," he observed with maddening calm. "I was merely making an observation. By the way," he added, his eyebrow quirked, "might I enquire what holds up the bodice of that dress? Sheer willpower?"

Tina jumped to her feet. "Do you want me to go and change?" she demanded. "Is that what you're saying?"

"God forbid!" He reached for a roll from the wicker basket, and broke off a chunk. "By all means wear that dress, Clementina, if it keeps you cool. Though I can hardly say the same for its effect on *my* temperature!"

Tina hesitated a moment, then sat down again. Why should she give him the satisfaction of forcing her into flight? With a poor appetite she spooned up the broth before her, though it was indeed delicious. A few sips of the cool white wine that Brant Wakefield poured for her helped to restore her equilibrium a little. When he rose to carve the joint of cold ham, which was to be accompanied by buttered new potatoes and a tossed green salad, she was able to answer his questions with relative composure.

He asked her about her parents, and Tina told him that they were both dead. "My father held the Chair in Social History at Bellchester," she explained.

"Very eminent!" Brant Wakefield commented, dark eyebrows raised. "And do you aspire to follow in his academic footsteps, Miss Harcourt?"

"Heavens no!" she laughed nervously. "Nothing so grand."

Brant held out a plate on which reposed two succulent slices of ham. As she took it from him their fingers made contact, and it was all Tina could do to hide the tremor that ran through her.

"So what *is* to be your destiny?" he enquired. "That is, after you have made your mark in the literary field with this book you're going to write for me."

More sarcasm? Or did he now believe that she *was* capable of the job she had been commissioned to do? When Tina gave him no answer, he suggested, "Marriage and babies, I suppose?" He shot her an assessing glance. "Is Dr. Charles Medwyn the man you have your sights on?"

Tina noted those arrogant lips of his curved in a cruelly ironic smile. How vastly surprised he would be, she thought, if she told him *yes*, that this was indeed the future laid out for her—marriage to Charles Medwyn. It was a union highly approved of by her family. By her father, before his death eighteen months ago, and by his sister, Tina's Aunt Ruth, who considered a mature and academically dedicated man like Charles the best sort of partner for a niece whom she suspected—as she never tired of reiterating—of having inherited the same shameless nature as her wanton mother.

Tina had crushed her instinctive rebellion at the idea of having her life decided for her, managing to convince herself that it was in her own best interests. Papa and Aunt Ruth were right, of course. Real love, true love, the only worthwhile kind of love, was the quiet emotion that she and Charles felt for one another. She knew she must sternly suppress those indefinable yearnings for a different sort of love—a love that carried one to peaks of bliss and was all-consuming in its demands. With Charles, she told herself repeatedly, she would ultimately achieve true fulfillment . . . a gentle, steady affection that would grow with time and sustain them both throughout their lives together.

Charles, it was already decided, would shortly be taking over the Chair of Social History at Bellchester, which old Professor Walters was keeping warm for him until the younger man was ready. Then he and Tina would celebrate their wedding in the time-graced college chapel, with the good wishes of the entire University ringing in joyful harmony with the sound of pealing bells. They would settle down to married life together in the mellow old house, set among Bellchester's dreaming spires, that went with Charles' appointment . . . the house in which Tina had spent her life until so recently, when, on her father's death, she and Aunt Ruth were obliged to vacate it in favour of the temporary new Professor, Gregory Walters. Her elderly aunt had retired to live out her days in a quiet country residential hotel in Cumberland, near her childhood home. And the twenty-one-year-old Tina had taken a bedsitter on the campus. For the first time she had tasted the sort of freedom taken for granted by the majority of undergraduates, and she had revelled in it. Fortunately, though, Charles' influence was there to help her curb any temptation to give way to the darker side of her nature which caused Tina so much anxiety and heartache.

Jerking her back to the present came Brant Wakefield's mocking voice, cutting across the silence in the gracious salon where the last rays of the setting sun glinted warmly on silver and crystal.

"You haven't answered my question, Clementina," he was admonishing her.

"I wish you wouldn't call me that," she muttered. He had made her hate the name which, in the past, she had always regarded with tolerant amusement.

His mouth quirked. "So it's not to be Blue Eyes, nor Clementina. Must we really stick to formality, Miss Harcourt?"

"I told you before, I'm usually known as Tina."

Slate-dark eyes gleamed. "Is that an invitation?"

"If you like," she shrugged, feeling cornered.

"So then, Tina," he went on remorselessly, "*have* you marriage designs on Dr. Charles Medwyn?"

Wouldn't the easiest thing be to tell him of the understanding she had with Charles? True, there was no official engagement as yet—Charles had suggested leaving this until her last term at Bellchester. But to all intents and purposes they were betrothed, and to say so straight out would put a stop to Brant Wakefield making easy game of her with his contemptuous remarks.

But for some obscure reason Tina held back. She felt almost afraid to explain the situation to this man, as if by putting her arrangement with Charles into definite, concrete words it would finalise everything, snapping the padlock on her future once and for all.

So instead, she temporised by saying, "Why should you assume that I want to marry him?"

"You mean that you don't?" he challenged, eyeing her intently through narrowed lids.

"I . . . er. . . ." Tina floundered. "Nothing is settled yet. Charles and I. . . ."

"What it amounts to," Brant declared, "is that you're keeping your options open, right? You've got this Charles Medwyn fellow nicely softened up, and you'll keep him that way unless someone even more eligible happens along?"

She threw him a chilling glance. "You seem to have a very low opinion of me, Mr. Wakefield."

"I wouldn't say that!" Lazily, he raised his glass and

held it in a beam of late sunlight so that the amber liquid glowed with an inner fire. "You are merely behaving like a true member of your sex."

"If that's your opinion of women," Tina returned scathingly, "then I pity the poor. . . ."

She choked off her words, but too late for him to miss their meaning. His dark eyes sparked at her across the dinner table, and somewhere in their depths was a gleam of triumph.

"I doubt if you need to spare your pity for the woman I choose as my bride," he jibed. "Taking into account this house and its three thousand acres, and all the extras that go with being the mistress of Hucclecote Hall! In addition to which, as icing on the cake, there is the income from a vast stretch of land down under, and ten thousand head of sheep. On the whole, I imagine, I'd be considered quite a catch for an ambitious woman."

"Is that what Loretta Boyd-French thinks?"

For a second time Tina wished she could snatch back her words, for he pounced with relish upon the opening she had offered him.

"I see you've wasted no time in doing your womanly homework."

"What's that supposed to mean?" she demanded.

"Isn't it something that all females learn at their mothers' knee," he drawled, "to check up on the elegibility of every passably handsome male that crosses their path?"

"You're just being ridiculous," Tina said hotly.

"Am I?" he countered, an expression of sweet reason on his handsome face. "Perhaps it was mere chance that you put my housekeeper through a virtual catechism about my marital status, almost the very first moment you arrived."

Hot waves of embarrassment swept over Tina, and

she wished that the floor would open up and swallow her.

"Has . . . has Mrs. Moncrieff been talking to you?" she asked faintly.

She felt like some tiny helpless creature before a cruel predator, too paralysed to summon the willpower to turn away from those steel-hard eyes that were gloating now with victory.

"She didn't need to tell me," he said with silky smoothness. "You'll have to learn, my dear Tina, to keep better control over your facial expressions if you want to hide your little feminine secrets." With that, Brant Wakefield rose to his feet and tossed down his napkin. "I'm afraid I have work to do now, so I'll say goodnight. There's a TV in the drawing room if you want some entertainment. Or a stereo, if you prefer music."

He was gone, and Tina was left alone with her thoughts. Five minutes later, when Mrs. Moncrieff came to enquire where Tina would like to take her coffee, she found that the girl who, only a few hours ago, had arrived brimming with confidence, for all her tender years, now appeared in very low spirits, with an air almost of defeat.

Chapter Three

In the drawing room, Tina found that she couldn't settle down to watch television. Even music, which normally she would have loved, seemed too disturbing for her fragile emotions this evening. The soaring strains of Dvorak's New World symphony made her eyes brim with wistful tears, and she switched it off at the end of the first movement.

Feeling restless, she wandered to the French windows which were thrown open to the balcony. The night air was a balm to her fevered skin, and smelled sweetly of summer blossoms. A flight of steps led downward to the ground level terrace and she descended slowly, holding the long skirt of her dress in one hand.

Tina was not intending to stroll far, just planning to make a circuit of the house before returning to her room to settle down with a book. But the tranquil summer night drew her further afield. Strolling on in the velvet darkness, she gazed up at the myriad stars that spangled the soft night sky. A silver crescent of moon lay low on the eastern horizon, shining through the lacework of branches of a massive cedar tree. All around her was the soft rustling of sleepy birds, and from somewhere far off a barn owl hooted. The whole earth seemed to be breathing in relief after the blazing heat of the day.

Presently, at the end of a paved footpath, she came to a wrought-iron gate set into a high stone wall. Her eyes had grown more accustomed to the darkness by now, and through the metalwork of the gate she discerned that this was a formally laid out garden, with shrubs and arbours and a central fountain, all enclosed within a rectangle of high walls. Drifts of honeysuckle reached her, to tangle sweetly with her senses.

Tina's probing fingers touched a latch and the gate swung open on smooth hinges. She wandered in and followed a flagged path through a rustic colonnade of early-flowering roses, whose blossoms gleamed palely in the faint moonglow. She reached out to touch one, stroking the slender petals with her fingertips and burying her small, upturned nose in its dewy centre to inhale the warm, musky fragrance. As she strolled on again she felt more exquisitely aware of natural beauty than ever before in her life, yet somehow her heart seemed heavy with an indefinable sadness. She came to the fountain, guided by the soft patter of water from its single moon-silvered jet. The wide rim of the stone basin offered her a seat and she allowed her fingers to trail in the water, tempted to splash its coolness over her burning face.

Suddenly, from somewhere nearby, she heard a man's smothered laugh and a girl's quick giggle. Tina froze in horror. A courting couple? A pair of lovers? If they spotted her here they would think she was some kind of Peeping Jill. Trying to move silently, keeping to the grassy edge of the path, she hastened back to the gate. Unfortunately, it had shut itself behind her, and she fumbled for the latch with impatient fingers. Failing to find it, she glanced around a little wildly. If she couldn't get the gate open she was trapped in here. She would have to admit her presence to the amorous couple, and ignominiously ask for their help in getting out.

Endeavouring to keep calm, Tina gave her careful attention to the gate once more. Darn it, where was the latch that she'd found so easily when entering? It seemed to have vanished into thin air. She gave vent to her feelings by gripping the fretted metalwork and shaking the gate hard.

"Open, you wretched thing!" she whispered furiously.

"Talking to gates now, are we?" drawled a voice from close at hand, giving Tina a nasty fright. "Well, it makes a change from talking to cars, I suppose."

Her face flamed, and she could only thank heaven that at least Brant Wakefield couldn't see her blush. Why did her rescuer have to be him, of all people?

"I can't open the gate," she explained in low tones.

"You managed to get it open to go in," he pointed out with maddening logic. "So what's the problem?"

"Well, er . . . the latch doesn't seem to be anywhere," Tina said foolishly.

"I assure you it most certainly is." She heard a click, and he went on in a condescending voice, as if to a small child, "You see, it hasn't really run away, as you seem to think. Gates may have ears, but latches don't usually possess a pair of legs!"

In her eagerness to get out, Tina gave the gate a hard push, but to her dismay it still wouldn't budge. She realised that Brant had let the latch fall back into place.

"What are you playing at?" she hissed at him through the metalwork.

"The question is rather, what are *you* playing at?" he countered. "You open this gate with the greatest of ease, linger inside the garden until I am conveniently passing, then pretend you can't get out. The well-worn helpless female ploy! You tried it this afternoon with your car, and now again."

His suggestion that she had deliberately engineered this situation took Tina's breath away.

"How was I to know that you'd be passing just at this minute?" she ground out furiously.

"Because," he argued, "you observed me setting off this way from the terrace. You decided that I must be going to the stable block, and would doubtless shortly be returning the same way."

She gasped in surprise, "You saw me just now on the terrace?"

"I did!"

"Well, I didn't see you," Tina denied flatly. "Now will you kindly let me out."

"What makes you so anxious to leave?" Brant debated. "It's a lovely evening, and one would have thought you'd enjoy being surrounded by the beauty of nature."

Tina dropped her voice to a mere whisper. "There's somebody in here," she explained. "A . . . a couple. . . ."

His soft chuckle was hateful to her, emphasizing, as it did, the extreme embarrassment of her position.

"I'm not in the least surprised," he observed drily. "This is an excellent place for a summer night's dalliance. It's one of the farmworkers and his sweetheart, I expect."

"Keep your voice down," she entreated, "or they'll hear you."

"Oh, I doubt that! I imagine they are both far too engrossed in one another to be aware of anything else."

"Mr. Wakefield, will you kindly open this gate immediately," Tina pleaded, on a note of desperation.

"By all means, Miss Harcourt. Your wish is my command!"

She should have been warned by his readiness to oblige. When she heard the latch click again and saw the gate swing back on its well-oiled hinges, she passed through the gap at a run, wanting only to get away from Brant Wakefield and hide herself in her room. But a powerful hand clamped down hard on her arm, and she found herself jerked round to face him.

"I thought I'd already taught you," he chided, "that one good turn deserves another."

Tina opened her mouth to remonstrate, but her objection was stifled by the sudden swift descent of his lips upon hers. She tried to struggle free but he drew her even closer, his arms becoming bands of steel that held their two bodies together, relentlessly moulding Tina's soft curves against his masculine hardness until her feeble resistance was swept away on a rising tide of sensual excitement which she had never experienced before. The blood throbbed wildly in her veins and she was lost in a spinning maelstrom of longing. His lips brushed fleetingly down across her smooth skin, seeking the secret hollows of her throat until Tina gave a reluctant little moan of delight, then moved on inexorably to the forbidden cleft between her swelling breasts which the low-cut dress revealed so indiscreetly. . . .

Then, from nowhere, like a camera shutter clicking, Tina had a split-second vision of Charles' face, his pale brown eyes wide with horror at such disgracefully abandoned behaviour in the woman he loved. The woman who was all-but engaged to be married to him. She went ice-cold, all emotion draining away in an instant. Then rage overwhelmed her, a storm of fury against this man who had so easily, so contemptuously, unlocked the shameful weakness that lay deep within her treacherous body.

Brant Wakefield sensed the change in her, and his hold relaxed. Seizing her chance, Tina raised her fists and pummelled the hard wall of his chest. But she failed to cause him the smallest physical hurt, so instead she attempted to wound him with the lash of her tongue.

"How dare you!" she denounced bitterly. "What sort of creature are you, to take advantage of a guest in your house in such a way? You're utterly despicable!"

His response was a scoffing laugh. "Take advantage! You were ready enough to be kissed, Clementina. In point of fact, it was precisely what you were angling for, wasn't it? You can't deny it."

"Of course I deny it!" Tina protested. "Just because you're so strong, and . . . and. . . ." She gulped, and tried again. "You seem to imagine that you've got some sort of God-given right to behave exactly as you choose."

"As Lord of the Manor, you mean?" he queried blandly. *"Droit de Seigneur,* and all that! Hmph! It would be quite an idea to revive that old custom. There are any number of pretty girls among the families on the estate, and if I can pick and choose among them as the whim takes me. . . ."

"Oh, you're impossible!" she choked. "I'm not going to stay here bandying words with you a moment longer."

Turning from him to hurry away, Tina felt his fingers close over her wrist like the talons of some cruel bird of prey, and she was spun violently back to face him again.

"Oh no you don't, Blue Eyes!" he ejaculated, and his voice was dangerous. "We're getting something straight before I let you run away."

"Let go of me," she cried. "You're hurting me."

"Stop snivelling," he barked. "I'm not in the habit of

treating women like fragile Dresden china; why should I? The members of your sex are a lot less pure and chaste than you like to make out. This 'taking advantage of me' nonsense, for instance. I wasn't kissing a cold stone slab just now, but a vibrant living woman who was enjoying it every bit as much as I was. So why not be honest and admit it, Miss Clementina Harcourt?"

"It's not true!" she sobbed, but quietly now, knowing that she was helpless in his grasp until he chose to release her. "You . . . you overpowered me, and there was nothing I could do."

"A girl who has the ability to kiss like that isn't the innocent little prude she pretends to be. She's had a fair amount of experience. Or was it," he added sneeringly, "just your natural instincts breaking out, despite yourself?"

Her natural instincts breaking out? He had hit the nail squarely on the head, and Tina shuddered in self-disgust. She begged him in a low voice, "Let me go, please!"

"Not until you admit that I'm right."

"You're not being fair," she whispered huskily. "Whatever happened to me just now . . . I wish with all my heart that it hadn't. You've got to believe that."

The cruel grip of his fingers eased slightly, but there was no pity in his words. "Were you scared that I wouldn't stop short at kissing, sweetheart? There's something you'd better get firmly into that pretty little head of yours! It's this—if you're not prepared for the consequences, then don't goad a man to the limit of his endurance."

"How . . . how can you possibly suggest that I goaded you?" she flared, her indignation returning in full force.

"Are you forgetting that sexy dress you're wearing?" he jeered. "That garment was expressly designed to fire a man's imagination . . . and I'm not lacking in that department! It cunningly reveals every seductive curve you possess . . . where it covers you at all. I've seen more discretion practised in a topless nightclub."

"I . . . I'll never wear the wretched thing again," she gasped on a sob.

"Is that meant as a promise?" he mocked. "Or as a threat?" He released her wrist and gave her a little push, one broad hand against her shoulder. "Get going, Clementina, before I change my mind and really give you what you deserve."

For a moment or two she was powerless to move, standing as if her feet were anchored to the ground by leaden weights. Brant Wakefield's face was lost in the shadows, but his eyes glittered like two dark pools.

"Mr. Wakefield," she managed at last, "if you expect me to remain in your house after this. . . ."

"That's up to you," he stated indifferently. "No doubt Dr. Charles Medwyn will be good enough to find someone else to replace you here, when I explain the circumstances of your hasty retreat."

"You . . . you mean you'd tell him?" she stammered, appalled.

"According to you, my dear Miss Harcourt, there's nothing to tell. So what are you so worried about?"

Tina felt reduced to silence. For a few moments longer she stood there irresolutely, wretchedly conscious that Brant Wakefield held the trump card. It wasn't so much that she feared he would really tell tales about her to Charles—even he couldn't be so vile, surely?—but because with all her heart she wanted to remain at Hucclecote Hall and carry out the job she'd been commissioned to do. The mere thought of leaving

here now filled her with an intolerable weight of
depression. And the reason for it—the awareness of the
spell that Brant Wakefield seemed to have cast over
her—caused Tina even greater distress.

At length, with a little sob she couldn't restrain, she
turned from him and fled back to the house.

Chapter Four

After a night of restless tossing and turning, of fevered dreams, Tina rose early and left the silent apartment by way of the outside steps leading down from the drawing room balcony. The coolness of the morning air was refreshingly welcome. Her whole body still felt sullied and bruised from the raw sensuality of that arrogant man, Brant Wakefield.

It was a morning of ineffable beauty, with sunlight filtering through the wraiths of mist that swirled in every tiny hollow, wrapping trees and bushes in gentle mystery. In one of the meadows Tina could see a herd of Jersey cows, newly freed from the milking parlour, frisking their tails and kicking up their legs like young calves. But around the house and immediate grounds all was slumbrous and still.

The shimmering crescent of the lake drew her like a magnet. As she crossed the smoothly undulating lawns, she paused a moment to slip off her sandals and turn up the flared bottoms of her jeans, then walked on again barefoot, the dew-laden grass deliciously cool between her toes. Away to the left a high bank of rhododendrons glowed with mist-muted colour, their huge blossoms in myriad shades of reds and pinks and purples, and purest virgin white. The honey-sweet scent of azaleas wafted gently towards her in the fresh morning air.

Watching a pair of swans gliding by in stately majesty, and mallards and shelducks and other water-fowl dodging in and out of the rushes with their young broods, Tina followed a footpath that skirted the lake to where the tip of the lake's crescent curled into a grove of silver birches. Here the sunlight came slanting down through the slender branches, making dappled patterns of light and shade. She paused yet again to gaze around her and breathe in the tranquil beauty. As she wandered on once more she was arrested by an unexpected sight. At the water's very edge, spotlighted by a bright beam of sun, was a magnificent golden stone Apollo poised on a plinth of rock.

Tina caught her breath in wondering admiration. Then, as she watched, the statue's arms came up slowly in preparation for a dive, palms meeting above the head. Her fanciful illusion was shattered in an instant, and she drew back quickly behind the shelter of a tree trunk, her pulses throbbing. This was no Greek God carved from cold stone, but a vibrant living male glorying in his strength and vitality. Brant Wakefield seemed to pause a timeless eternity, and Tina could not tear her gaze from his superb naked figure, though her whole body tingled with heightened colour. Her eyes drank him in, awed by the sheer force of virile masculinity . . . the proudly lifted head, the breadth of shoulder and moulded power of chest and arms, the hard flat stomach and tapered hips, the secret loins and muscled thighs and calves. . . .

It was something of a shock when he suddenly moved, thrusting forward in a dive that speared the limpid water with hardly a splash. He began swimming in a fast crawl, and every stroke brought him nearer to where Tina stood watching. In a panic, she shrank back behind the concealing tree until her courage broke and she turned and fled, racing all the way back to the sanctuary of the house. It was only when she reached the sweep of gravel that she became wincingly aware of her barefoot state, and paused to slip on her sandals.

An aroma of coffee greeted her when she re-entered the apartment. Mrs. Moncrieff appeared in the kitchen doorway.

"Good morning, lassie," she smiled pleasantly. "I saw you running across the grass. Working up a nice appetite for your breakfast, were you?"

"Oh, no, not really. . . ." Tina stammered, still feeling flustered. "I . . . I just. . . ."

"How about a piece of finnan haddock and a poached egg?" the housekeeper suggested. "Start the day right, that's what I always say."

"Oh no, I couldn't, thanks very much." Tina's stomach had clenched at the mere thought of such food. "Just coffee and toast and marmalade—that's all I want."

Mrs. Moncrieff shook her head doubtfully. "You young lassies, you don't eat enough to keep a wee fly alive. Mr. Brant now, he's a man worth cooking for!"

"Will I be breakfasting with him?" Tina asked, trying to conceal her alarm.

"I doubt that! He'll have been out and about for ages, and he rarely gets back before nine."

Relief washed over her at the housekeeper's words. She'd have to face Brant Wakefield soon enough, but the intimacy of a shared meal at this moment was more than she could endure. She would be too uncomfortably aware of the scene at the lakeside just now, and knew that her face would flame betrayingly each time those slate-grey eyes of his met hers. Moreover, there was the embarrassing encounter last night by the gate to the walled garden. Would he refer to that again, Tina wondered, or would he have the common decency to let it remain behind a cloak of silence?

She hurried through her own breakfast, served in a small bright sun-room open to a flat roof, with white table and chairs and vivid orange scatter-cushions. She managed only one small triangle of toast and two restoring cups of good hot coffee. Then, having changed into a dark brown skirt and a plain cotton blouse (to look as severe and businesslike as possible), she told Mrs. Moncrieff that if Mr. Wakefield should want to know where she was, she would be in the library, making a preliminary survey.

Once she had found her way to the elegant, book-lined room downstairs, Tina soon became absorbed. Each volume of family records she pulled at random from the shelves told her that she would find a wealth of material on which to base her history of the Wakefields. Their origins stretched back to the time of William the Conqueror. They had, it seemed, always been fiercely loyal to the Crown, proud and trenchant traditionalists. Like all great families, they'd had their fair share of good and bad . . . the high-principled Wakefields who'd treated their tenants and peasantry with justice and generosity, the occasional black sheep who had neglected the estate and squandered money in gambling and womanising.

Tina flitted here and there through the centuries, building a rough framework in her mind from which to begin her more detailed research. Eagerly, she turned the pages describing ancient events, jotting notes on the pad that she kept beside her. Bent over the huge desk topped with gold-tooled leather, she didn't hear the library door open, and she wasn't aware of the footsteps that made little sound on the stretch of oriental carpet.

"Hard at it, I see," said a deep voice from right

behind her. She spun around to find Brant Wakefield's lean-chiselled face only inches from her own. She stood up hastily and stepped back to put a little distance between them.

"I . . . I'm sorry, Mr. Wakefield, but I didn't hear you come in," she faltered.

"We seem to be in the habit of stumbling upon one another unawares," he replied obscurely.

"What . . . what do you mean?"

He shrugged, not deigning to answer her directly. Instead, he went off at a tangent. "It was marvellous in the water this morning. You should have tried it yourself."

Tina was appalled by the implication of those words, but she strove to remain cool and collected. In a voice of false innocence, she enquired, "Have you been swimming, then?"

His eyes mocked her. "Come now, you can surely do better than that? Why ask a question to which you already know the answer?"

Flushing scarlet, Tina decided it was useless to go on pretending, if Brant had actually seen her there in the birch wood. So she tried the next best thing, throwing out carelessly, "Oh, that was you in the lake, was it? I saw a head bobbing in the water, and I didn't realise. . . ."

"You saw a damn sight more than just a head!"

Tina wished to heaven that the floor would open up and swallow her; that a thunderbolt would strike or some other dire emergency occur. *Anything,* she thought wildly, to put an end to this inquisition.

"Shouldn't we be getting on with some work?" she faltered, and glanced meaningfully at her wristwatch. "I'm sure you must have great demands on your time."

He ignored that. "Perhaps tomorrow you'd care to join me in the lake," he suggested. "Shall we say seven-thirty? A quick dip first thing really sets you up for the day, you know."

What devil's pleasure he got from taunting her, Tina realised miserably. "Thank you, but I would rather not," she managed in a coldly formal voice. "Swimming is not my strong suit. Now, Mr. Wakefield, you've commissioned me to write a book for you, so hadn't you better allow me to get on with it?"

"As you wish," he said stiffly, and went to a large carved oak chest standing in one corner of the room. Lifting the lid, he revealed a cavernous interior that appeared to be stacked deep with bundles of papers, many of them yellowed with great age.

"I imagine everything is in here . . . the saga of the Wakefield family and Hucclecote Hall. But it will all need sorting first. Would you like me to lay on some assistance? I could always get a secretarial agency to send along a temp."

"No," said Tina quickly. "I'd prefer to manage by myself. It's quicker in the end."

"Have it your own way," he shrugged. "I can spare an hour now, to help you get launched, and we can have another go at it this evening. You'd better take some time off this afternoon in lieu," he added off-handedly.

Brant started lifting out packages, and together they began to get them sorted into a roughly chronological order. He was briskly practical, and despite the tension which Tina couldn't forget for a single minute, she found that they worked together well. Absorbed in a fascinating series of documents which told the story of how, three hundred years ago, a younger son had been disinherited for daring to marry the woman of his choice, a mere apothecary's daughter, neither of them heard the sound of a car scrunching to a sportive halt on the apron of gravel outside. A few minutes later the library doors burst open impetuously to admit a tall and very attractive blond girl. Tina and Brant happened to be bent over the desk together, heads close as they deciphered faded ink on yellowed parchment, and they both glanced up in surprise.

A pair of sparking violet eyes met Tina's blue ones in a challenging stare. Tina knew without doubt who this was, and she felt a curiously hollow feeling of despair as she registered the other girl's slender loveliness. Her slacks and country-casual tweed jacket were impeccably cut to show off her slim shapely figure to the best advantage, and her poise and bearing had the assured stamp of one born to the purple.

Dismissing Tina contemptuously, she advanced upon Brant with a little cry of delight.

"Darling, Mrs. Moncrieff told me you were down here." She slid her hands up round his neck and tilted her face to offer him the enticement of her sensually curved lips.

Smiling down at her, Brant kissed her briefly. "It's great to see you, Loretta. I thought you and your father were staying in London for at least another week."

"We are," she confirmed, "but Daddy had to return home for a couple of days to sort out some disagreement or other on the local council. So, since you've refused to take time off to come and visit me in London, I decided to come back with him to see *you*. How's that for devotion, Brant darling? Daddy and I only arrived home half an hour ago, and I've come rushing straight over here without even stopping to change my clothes. Now, you're to drop everything and we'll go riding or something."

"I only wish I could," he told her regretfully, "but I've got an expert on Folk Museums arriving any minute. He's coming to advise me on opening up the old craft workshops again, and I'll have to spend the rest of the day with him."

Loretta pouted prettily. "Oh well, I suppose it can't be helped! This evening then . . . you must come to dinner at the Manor."

Brant shook his head. "Unfortunately, I've arranged to spend the evening working here with Tina. I wasn't expecting to see you today."

The violet eyes pinpointed to cold amethyst. "Tina?"

"Oh, you haven't been introduced, have you?" he said easily. "Tina, this is Loretta Boyd-French. Loretta, meet Miss Harcourt. She's going to write the history of the Wakefield family. I told you about it, remember?"

"I believe you did mention something or other," the girl said negligently. "But you'll have to make other arrangements, Brant. You *must* come to dinner tonight. Daddy is expecting you."

He hesitated, looking doubtful. "It will hold Tina up unless I show her the way around all these old family records," he explained. "She can't really get started until we've got them sorted out a bit."

Loretta's laugh tinkled in the lightest kind of scorn. "If Miss Harcourt is held up, darling, it's your money that's wasted, not hers." She wound her arms seductively round his neck again, and Tina noted with a little shiver the way her slender fingers curled into his hair. "Come on, Brant, don't be a meanie. Heavens above, I've been away a whole week!"

He smiled again, and gave way. "All right, then, I'll be glad to come to dinner this evening." He glanced at Tina. "We'll have to leave things over until tomorrow as I really have no more time to spare now. Come on, Loretta, let's have a drink upstairs before this chap arrives, and you can tell me what you've been up to in London this past week."

As the doors closed behind the two of them, Tina heard that silvery laugh tinkle again, and she felt a spurt of fury at the way Loretta had interrupted their working session. Without Brant Wakefield's magnetic presence in the library she felt strangely bereft, and try as she might she could not settle back to work again. The ancient family documents, which only a few minutes ago she had found so vitally interesting, somehow failed to hold her attention.

It must have been twenty minutes later that, in her restless prowling about the room, Tina wandered to one of the mullioned windows. What she espied just outside made her draw back hastily. Only a few feet away from her, standing by the bonnet of a long, low, racy-looking sports car, were the two people who had been haunting her mind. They were locked together in a tight embrace, arms entwined around each other. Observing them covertly, Tina found herself hating this girl who could bend Brant Wakefield to her bidding with a few flashes of her violet eyes and the cajoling note in her huskily attractive voice.

By noon, Tina's head ached and she was in desperate need of fresh air. She went for a stroll in the grounds and wandered along an avenue of ancient chestnut trees, their great ribbed trunks writhing up to spread a cool green canopy of foliage above her head.

When she returned to the house for lunch, slightly refreshed, she found she was expected to eat with Brant and his visitor, who was introduced to her as Mr. Jocelyn Ashley. He was a pleasant looking man whom she judged to be around forty, but he seemed much younger because of his almost boyish enthusiasm for his job.

"I say, Miss Harcourt, you really do know your stuff!" he exclaimed admiringly at one point. They had been discussing the subject of serfdom on medieval estates, while consuming the delicious salmon soufflé Mrs. Moncrieff had served to them as the first course. "Brant is going to find you very useful to have around when he makes a start with setting up his various workshops."

"Oh, but I don't expect to be here that long," Tina protested. "I'm only staying at Hucclecote Hall to do the necessary research for my book."

"That's a pity! I'm sure your help would be invaluable to him in all sorts of ways," Jocelyn Ashley opined.

Tina tried to stem the rush of colour to her cheeks as she felt Brant's eyes turn toward her in contemplative appraisal.

"I agree, Clementina certainly knows her stuff," he said ambiguously. "She has a remarkable grasp of things for one so young."

Jocelyn Ashley appeared to notice nothing of the *frisson* that hung in the air between his two luncheon companions. He rattled on happily, "I wonder if you've ever been to the Weald and Downland Museum, Miss Harcourt? It's not all that far from here, and it really is a most fascinating place. As an open-air museum it's quite splendidly laid out, and for someone like you whose special subject is Social History it's a must, I'd say."

Tina replied smilingly, "I've heard about it, of course, and I was planning to fit in a visit while I'm here."

"Perhaps we could go together, Tina?"

She glanced round quickly at this unexpected suggestion from Brant, only to find an enigmatic expression on his face. Was this more of his taunting, or did he mean it seriously?

Luncheon over, the two men went off to see an old Sussex barn being renovated for use as a tannery—tanning had been a thriving craft at Hucclecote Hall as little as a century ago. Brant had it in mind to carry the leather-making process right through to the manufacture of fine saddlery and riding boots . . . a lucrative sideline to help balance the budget, as well as provide an additional show-piece for the visitors who came to Hucclecote Hall.

Tina returned to the library and forced herself to concentrate on work. The chair just beside her, which Brant had occupied this morning, was a constant reminder of his absence now, and she sat with closed eyes, fighting off the dark longings which she fervently wished she could deny.

What sort of girl are you, Tina Harcourt? she asked herself wretchedly. The first time you encounter a sensual man like Brant Wakefield, a man with earthy, untamed passions, you're consumed by a raging inferno of emotional excitement. With a couple of lustful kisses, in which tenderness played no part at all, he's exposed you for the cheap little wanton that deep down you really are.

At least, she determined with gritted teeth, Brant would never have the satisfaction of knowing the truly terrifying power of those wild urges he had unleashed in her. There would be no further abandonment of the high principles which her father and Aunt Ruth had taught her to hold dear . . . the principles which governed her relationship with Charles.

She spent a wretched afternoon and evening. Dining in solitary state, Tina could imagine the scene at Maddehurst Manor with searing clarity, for only recently she had admired photographs of the house and its interior in a new illustrated book on English Manor Houses that she'd come across in the University library:

the panelled dining room, with the Boyd-French's heraldic shield above the great stone hearth; the massive refectory table of polished oak, on which the pointed flames of a dozen candles would shed their cool, pellucid light. And Loretta, beautifully gowned to show off her seductive figure, darting provocative glances at the dark-haired man opposite her; the pair of them smiled upon benignly by her noble father, Viscount Boyd-French.

Tina's knife and fork clattered on the plate as unbidden tears filled her eyes. The housekeeper, entering with dessert, glanced at her with concern.

"Has something upset you, lassie?" she enquired.

"Nothing," Tina lied transparently. "I'm just tired, that's all."

Mrs. Moncrieff frowned severely at the barely tasted grilled Dover sole reposing on Tina's plate.

"You'll make yourself really ill if you don't eat your meals," she scolded, then added coaxingly, "Now let me tempt you to try a little of this caramel pudding. Good eggs and cream it's made of. Do you the world of good!"

Tina nodded listlessly, and swallowed a spoonful or two under Mrs. Moncrieff's watchful eye.

She retired early with a book, but found herself re-reading the same paragraph for the umpteenth time. At length, feeling stifled, she slid out of bed and wandered to the window. The little balcony afforded room enough for her to step outside and escape the sultriness of the house. The night air struck a welcome coolness to her skin through her filmy nightdress, and she leant against the stone balustrade listening to the sounds that came to her out of the darkness . . . the deep, full-throated song of a nightingale in the ash grove beyond the stable block . . . the sonorous striking of eleven from the tower clock of the private chapel . . . and drifting across the meadows the faint sounds of men's voices raised in song—estate workers returning home in a jolly mood from the village pub, she guessed. All the gentle sounds of a peaceful summer night. The stars were heavy, dripping their light from a velvet sky. The air was elusively redolent of a hundred mingled scents.

From far off came the droning of a motor, growing louder. A car was entering the park gates, approaching the house along the curving driveway. Brant, home this early? Unlikely. All the same Tina's breath was bated until the car turned off at the garages in the old stable block. Then silence returned. Perhaps it had been the estate bailiff, Jeff Lintott, whose farmhouse was near the stables.

Tina fell back into a reverie. Then she snapped to full alertness at the sound of a footstep just below. About to retreat to her room, she froze. Better, perhaps, to remain quite still, then she wouldn't be seen. She was thankful that only a shaded bedside lamp was on, shedding a faint glow that was hardly sufficient to illuminate her out here.

The footsteps stopped, and to her horror Brant's voice floated up to her.

"Can't you sleep, Clementina?" he enquired softly.

That wretched name again, used only in mockery! Useless not to reply, she decided, so she murmured through the sudden huskiness in her throat, "I just came out for a breath of air. It's stifling tonight."

"Why not come down then," he suggested, "and we'll have a stroll. There'll be a breeze across the lake, there always is."

"Oh no, I can't!"

"Can't?" he tossed back at her sharply.

"I . . . I'm just going to get back into bed," she amended.

"Better a bed of hay beneath the stars, Clementina," he poeticised.

"How many times must I ask you not to call me that?" she said unsteadily.

"What's in a name?" he quoted lightly. *"That which we call a rose, by any other name would smell as sweet."* He paused, then added musingly, "You know, you might well be Juliet yourself, up there on your balcony in that diaphanous nightgown, with your hair tumbled about your shoulders."

"And you cast yourself in the role of Romeo, the amorous swain?" she countered, trying to match him in his own brand of sarcasm.

"Why not? I have all the necessary . . . attributes."

"I only hope Loretta thinks so," she threw down, amazed at her own temerity. It must be the distance that separated them, twenty feet of vertical stone wall, that gave her a feeling of safety.

Brant's voice sounded dangerous as he said, "Let's leave Loretta out of this conversation."

"I'm happy to," she riposted. "In fact, I think it's more than time that, like Juliet, I say goodnight till it be morrow."

There was a short silence in which Tina foolishly imagined she had scored against him. Then he remarked chattily, "You know, I always thought that Shakespeare made Romeo rather a feeble fellow not to have him clambering up to his lady love for at least a goodnight kiss, on that first evening he stood around swooning beneath her balcony."

"He would have to have been a steeplejack for that," Tina pointed out, "before he arranged with the nurse to lower a rope ladder for him."

"Think so?" Brant retorted, and to her consternation Tina heard a scrambling noise from below. She wanted to flee back into the safety of her room and shut the window against him, but she decided that it would only cause him greater amusement. So she stood her ground, quaking inwardly.

In a very few moments, Brant's head appeared above the balustrade. Another second and he agilely swung one of his long legs over and leapt down beside her. His dark eyes glittered in the faint light coming from within the room.

"Well now, Juliet, have I earned that kiss?" he demanded.

"Don't . . . don't be silly," she faltered. "How did you get up here so easily, anyway?"

"A convenient growth of ivy," he explained.

Trying desperately to conceal her violent shivering from him, Tina ordered, "Well then, you can either go back the same way, or straight out through my door, if you prefer. But whichever way, please be quick about it."

"That kiss, first!" he said threateningly.

"No!" she cried, stepping back quickly.

But what escape had she? Retreat into her room, where Brant could follow? Her *bedroom!* She shuddered at the thought and remained on the balcony, facing him as bravely as she could. He gave a soft laugh, deep in his throat, and then she was gathered into his arms. His kiss surprised Tina with its gentleness, a mere touching of his lips to hers, while his fingertips slid across the warm flesh of her shoulders. A tremor ran through her, and Brant must have felt it. Suddenly his grip tightened and he drew her closer to him with the same bruising intensity he had used last night in the garden. Tina's zephyr-thin nightdress formed no barrier between them and she was intensely, swooningly aware of every hard contour of his body, the throbbing urgency of his maleness. Her lips parted of their own volition under his warm, searching tongue, and she could feel his hands moulding the soft, pliant curves of her body until desire soared within her and she was swept away into a sweet, delirious, lost world where only the senses counted.

Abruptly, his hands ceased their fevered roaming and his grip slackened. He eased himself back from her and looked down into the dark pools of her eyes.

"Tina, I . . . ."

Strangely, inexplicably, it was the note of hesitant uncertainty in his voice that brought awareness screaming back to Tina. What madness had possessed her, to allow him such intimacy at nearly midnight on the balcony of her bedroom, and she dressed only in this filmy, revealing nightdress?

She tore away from his loosened grasp and flung at him in bitter accusation, "You must be mad, insane, behaving like this! Get out of my room this instant, and don't you ever dare to so much as touch me again."

Brant had recovered an iron mastery of himself, it seemed, if not yet total composure. The smoky passion of his dark grey eyes had given way to sparking fire.

"Protesting your sweet girlish innocence again?" he drawled. "You've got a nerve, Clementina!"

"Get going!" she ordered, her own eyes blazing.

For a moment longer he stood there in utter stillness, a muscle twitching in his jaw, and she trembled before the sheer fury in his expression. Then he stepped through the French windows into her room, and moved swiftly across to the door in a few long strides. There he paused and glanced back at her.

"Get this into your head, here and now," he gritted harshly, and the knuckles on his clenched fists gleamed whitely. "Once I'm gone, you'll have no need to lock your door against me. Not tonight or any other night. You'll be left to enjoy your maidenly peace."

Tina stood mutely by the window, her hands folded across her breast in a concealing gesture. Seeing his features twisted into a bitter smile, she felt herself go cold as if fingers of ice had touched her.

"Sweet dreams, Clementina," he jeered hatefully. Then he left the room without another glance. And the fact that he closed the door gently behind him was infinitely worse than if he had slammed out in a raging temper.

Chapter Five

Two days later—two days of tight-lipped tension whenever their paths crossed—Brant departed for London.

Running after Loretta, thought Tina grimly, despite having told her that he couldn't spare any time off to go to London. The lovely Loretta had only to lift one of her slender fingers to make him do whatever she wanted!

Without Brant's presence, the great house seemed silent as a tomb. Tina was depressingly aware that she wasn't making much progress with her research work. Constantly, while sitting at the huge leather-topped desk in the library, she found herself in a daydream, her wayward thoughts wandering along forbidden paths.

The weather grew hotter than ever and Tina sweltered even in the lightest and skimpiest of her summer dresses. She was thankful, at least, that her scant clothing wouldn't draw sarcastic comments from the absent Brant. On the second afternoon he was away, she gave up trying to do any serious work and wandered outside with a book to find a shady spot. The lake enticed her with its coolness, and presently she found herself in the birch grove once more. She moved to the water's edge, reaching the point where an outcrop of rock made a convenient diving platform.

She stepped up on it, and stood where Brant had stood that morning, magnificently naked. She glanced towards the tree behind which she had hidden and realised blushingly how little concealment it afforded from this angle. He must have been aware of her presence the entire time.

Hearing someone approaching along the path through the trees, Tina spun around quickly. She was relieved to see the friendly face of Jeff Lintott, Brant's bailiff.

"Wishing you'd got a swimsuit with you, Miss Harcourt?" he greeted her. "That nice clear water looks really inviting on a sultry day like this, doesn't it?"

Tina was glad to have her presence here explained away like that. "Yes," she agreed, giving an envious sigh, "but it hardly seems worth making myself hotter than ever by going back to the house to fetch one."

"I wonder . . . would you care to join me for a cup of tea?" he invited, and there was a faintly wistful look on his pleasant, weathered face. "My farmhouse is only a couple of hundred yards away if we cut through the wood."

She felt sorry for Jeff. Mrs. Moncrieff had told her how, after only a couple of years of blissfully happy married life, his attractive young wife had been killed by a drunken driver while she was shopping in a nearby town. Since that tragedy, Jeff had lived the lonely life of a widower for more than three years.

"A cup of tea is just what I could do with," she smiled warmly.

As they fell into step together along the woodland path, Tina enquired, "Does this mean that you've finished work for the day?"

"Heavens no!" Jeff made a wry face. "With the amount there is to do getting things properly shipshape here, the hours of daylight simply aren't long enough. I'll be hard at it right through until about ten o'clock this evening, I expect."

"Poor you!" she sympathised.

"Oh, don't get me wrong, I thrive on work! In fact . . ." A shadow flitted across his face. ". . . it's hard work that keeps me going."

"From something I overheard the other day," Tina said, hoping to please him, "I gather that Mr. Wakefield has a very high opinion of your capabilities."

"It's mutual," he responded. "Brant's a great guy, with the sort of drive and enthusiasm this place needs just now."

They had reached the gate of the farmhouse—a charming building that in its much smaller way echoed the architectural style of the Hall. In the cluttered, low-ceilinged room that served Jeff as kitchen, living-room, dining-room *et al*, he filled the electric kettle and plugged it in, then got out crockery and a cake tin. While doing so he enlarged upon his theme.

"Brant is determined to get this estate back on its feet in double quick time," he told Tina. "In his uncle's day, things were allowed to run down badly. I used to try and persuade old man Sebastian to consider some innovations like opening the house to the public and using modern farming methods for greater efficiency. But he flatly refused to listen. It's all happening now, though, with Brant!"

"I gather it was only because of a tragic accident that he ever inherited," Tina remarked probingly.

"That's right. The first in line was Sebastian's son, Richard, but he was killed last summer when he crashed his sports car in the South of France." Pouring water into the teapot, Jeff cast her a sidelong glance. "Don't get me wrong, Miss Harcourt, but . . . well,

Richard would never have done what Brant is doing. Frankly, he liked enjoying himself too much."

They were silent for a few moments while Tina digested this information. Then she said hesitantly, "I heard that Loretta Boyd-French was engaged to Richard Wakefield."

Jeff's expression clouded. "It does shake you a bit," he agreed, not even pretending that he hadn't followed her own train of thought. "I'm a romantic, like you must be, and it's not my idea of the perfect match for Brant. Still, looked at from the point of view of the families concerned, I suppose it's a good enough arrangement. Her side has the right sort of aristocratic connections, while Brant's got the wealth that the Boyd-French clan lacks. Morever," Jeff added, "Loretta is right here and handy, and he hasn't all that much time to find himself a wife."

The cup rattled in the saucer as Tina took it from him. "What makes you say that?" she asked, with feigned casualness.

Jeff had the cake tin open and was offering her a choice of its contents. "Agnes Moncrieff keeps me well supplied with goodies," he explained with a grin. "She thinks I'd fade away without her shortbread and bannock cake etcetera."

Selecting the smallest piece of shortbread she could find, Tina had to repeat her question. "Why does Mr. Wakefield have to find a wife in a hurry?"

"Terms of the inheritance," Jeff explained, taking a Scotch pancake for himself. "It's been laid down for generations that the incumbent at Hucclecote Hall has to be wed by the time he's reached thirty-five, or he forfeits all his rights and claims. Brant's got less than a year to go now, so he can't afford to waste any time."

Tina felt shocked to the core. What sort of man was

Brant Wakefield that he could calmly take on the woman who had been betrothed to his recently dead cousin simply to fulfill a legal requirement for the continued enjoyment of his legacy? In his eyes, no doubt, Loretta had the advantage of being readily available, and already stamped with the seal of approval as a fitting wife for a Wakefield heir. But what about *love?* Wasn't that supposed to enter into it somewhere?

Jeff was regarding her curiously. "You must surely have come across such arrangements often enough in your line of research?" he said. "I mean to say, the old landed families used to keep things within a very tight circle, and there was rarely any marrying outside it."

She nodded. "I know, but it seems different somehow when the participants are merely names you come across in old historical documents."

But Jeff was right, this was just one more marriage of convenience, without any pretence of feelings of love between the two parties. She had no difficulty in believing that Loretta Boyd-French was capable of marrying purely for money and the right status. And as for Brant . . . hadn't he made his sweeping contempt for womenkind crystal clear? To a man of his ilk, love was something that had no meaning. Only lust. She could imagine him reciting scornfully with that infuriatingly arrogant expression of his, "A woman is a woman is a woman."

Jeff, seeing that she was upset, though without really understanding the reason for it, discreetly changed the subject.

"It must be a bit lonely for you at the moment, all on your own in the big house." He gave her a tentative smile. "I'm afraid there's not much I can suggest, considering that I'm working all the hours God sends! Still, how about dropping in with me at the village pub for the last half hour before closing time tonight? You need jollying up a bit."

"Thanks, Jeff," she said, shaking her head. "But I don't think. . . ."

"Come on, say yes," he coaxed. "You never know, you might pick up some useful information from some of the elderly locals. At least three of the pub's regulars are well into their eighties."

Why not? Tina thought. It was true that she was lonely . . . she had never in her life felt more isolated than now. Perhaps Jeff and some of the villagers at the pub would help assuage her longing for company.

"Okay, I'll be glad to come," she told him with a smile.

Next day, by arrangement, Tina again joined Jeff for a cup of tea in his farmhouse. When she got back to the library, at about five-thirty, she found Brant there. He seemed in the very devil of a rage.

"Where have you been?" he demanded gruffly.

Although her heart had been thrown into a flutter at the sight of Brant, she faced up to him squarely, and retorted, "Is that any business of yours?"

"I employ you, don't I?"

"You employ me, Mr. Wakefield, to carry out a certain assignment. Not to work fixed hours."

There seemed to be real hatred in the look he turned on her. "Must you always be so pert in your answers?"

"Must you always be so rude in your questions?" she countered.

His jaw clenched grimly and Tina felt a little scared of his anger. But he managed to control it, and ground out, "You've been with Jeff Lintott at the farmhouse, haven't you? And last night, so I hear, you went to the local pub with him. This is a new development!"

"If you knew where I've been," she commented sweetly, "why did you ask? I seem to recall that a few days ago you reprimanded me for posing questions to which I already knew the answer."

A flame burned in the recesses of his slate-grey eyes. He strode to a window and stood staring out, arms folded implacably across his broad chest.

"How is your work going?" he enquired abruptly.

"Oh, fine!" she lied.

"Tomorrow," he stated after a moment, in a tone that brooked no denial, "we'll go to that open air museum that Jocelyn Ashley mentioned."

Tina sternly suppressed the excitement that leapt within her. "I'm sorry," she said coldly, "but tomorrow I'll be too busy."

He turned to look at her, his face a blank mask. "Busy? With what, precisely?"

"Er . . . I'm digging out some facts about the Wakefields' involvement in the Dissolution of the Monasteries," she embroidered with only the thinnest thread of truth.

"That can wait," he said brusquely. "Tomorrow, then. Be ready at ten o'clock."

Dismayed, Tina watched him cross to the door in a few long strides. Then he was gone, without so much as a backward glance. She dreaded the thought of spending the day with him, yet how could she refuse? As long as she continued in this job, Brant Wakefield was her boss and his word was law.

For the first time in weeks the morning sky was clouded. As they spun through the Sussex lanes in Brant's white Mercedes, hugging the rounded contours of the South Downs, Tina heard an occasional mutter of thunder coming from across the English Channel. Fortunately, when they reached the Weald and Downland Museum the rain was still holding off, but the threat of it had kept the number of visitors down to a minimum.

It was the perfect setting for such a place, Tina thought, as she surveyed the beautiful little parkland valley in which the unique collection was gathered. Dotted all around were various medieval buildings which, scheduled for demolition because of road widening and so on, had been re-erected here to preserve them for future generations. Brant studied each of the exhibits with keen interest, asking intelligent questions of the volunteer attendants about methods of construction and original usage. But the sky was lowering all the time, and just as they reached the Charcoal Burners' encampment, deserted in its woodland clearing, the clouds suddenly broke and the rain came pelting down. With no other shelter nearby, Brant pushed Tina into the tiny, turf-covered hut in which the old-time charcoal burners and their families had lived their lives. It was dark and cramped inside, and they sat together on one of the crudely-constructed benches that must have served as a bed.

"This may be somewhat primitive," Brant observed amusedly, "but you can't say it isn't pleasantly intimate." His mood this morning seemed to have been improving in contrast to the deterioration of the weather.

"We can't stay here long," Tina murmured uneasily.

"Why not?" was the bland reply. "I have no engagements for the rest of the day—and," he added with a soft chuckle, "I'm not short of ideas on how we could pass the time."

Tina drew away from him in instinctive alarm. To channel his thoughts into another, safer direction, she enquired, "Did you enjoy yourself in London?"

She sensed him freeze, his body going rigid. But his voice was calm . . . dangerously calm.

"Why should you want to know, Clementina?"

What was the good, she thought, of constantly protesting about him calling her by that name?

"I was just asking," she said lamely.

"Have you been wishing that you were with me?" he hazarded.

"Certainly not! Why should I?"

"You might have found it lonely in my absence," he explained. Then, "But I was forgetting, you consoled yourself with Jeff Lintott, didn't you?"

"This is ridiculous," she flared, grateful that it was too dim in the hut for him to see her face, "Why shouldn't I have a chat with Jeff if I want to? Do I have to ask *your* permission?"

"Or Charles'?" he suggested. "Would he be happy, do you think, about how you've been employing your leisure time?"

Charles! Guiltily, Tina realised that she'd scarcely given him a thought these past days. But then, she and Charles understood one another. He had never shown the least objection when she had attended Students' Union dances without him. Dancing was not exactly his thing, he'd explained repeatedly, and besides it was hardly dignified for someone in his position to be seen jigging around. Charles had known that she was normally escorted home from these "hops" by one or another of the male students, and if she'd not seen fit to mention their experimental attempts at love-making . . . well, it was because it had meant less than nothing to her.

With Jeff Lintott there wasn't even the most innocent kiss to feel guilty about, nor ever would be, Tina felt sure. Then suddenly her whole body flushed with hot colour as she remembered the burning kisses of this man beside her now. Never in a million years would someone like Charles be able to understand the tormenting flame that Brant Wakefield had ignited in her with such contemptuous ease.

But not ever again, she vowed to herself, and moved another few inches away from the man who, by his very nearness, by the undeniable aura of virility that he exuded, could dominate her thoughts and set fire to her senses.

Brant was remarking chattily, "You'll soon find out how Charles feels about your dalliancing. You'll have the chance to confess all when you see him this weekend."

"There's no question of my seeing Charles this weekend," Tina denied, though a curious feeling of anxiety took hold of her.

"Oh, didn't I tell you?" Brant's voice was insidiously smooth. "He phoned you when you were visiting Jeff Lintott at the farmhouse yesterday. I told him that—at any rate as far as your research was concerned— everything was going well, and I invited him to come for the weekend to see for himself. It just so happens that his team are moving their base this weekend, so he was able to accept. He'll be at Hucclecote Hall in time for lunch tomorrow." Brant paused, then before Tina had time to gather her scattered wits, he added, "Won't that be pleasant for you both? You'll be able to bring him up-to-date on . . . everything that's been happening to you."

Tina finally found her voice, though it came out sounding tight and husky. "What's your game?" she demanded furiously. "What are you trying to do to me?"

"I assure you it's no game," he responded. And after

a moment's pause, "It doesn't sound to me as if you're altogether pleased at the prospect of seeing your . . . how shall we describe him? Your fiancé?"

"Charles is not my fiancé," she objected.

"What would he say, I wonder, to hear you leaping in with such a forceful denial?" Brant jibed. "I imagine that Dr. Medwyn believes that it's all agreed between you, bar the formalities."

As Tina gripped her hands tightly together in silent fury, her nails digging into her palms, Brant enquired in a deceptively soft voice, "Are you having doubts, Clementina?"

"Of course I'm not having doubts," she insisted vehemently. Rising to her feet she edged around his long legs in the confined space so that she could peer out of the rude doorway. "Shall we go now? I think the rain has slackened off."

"Don't be absurd, it's still pelting cats and dogs," he retorted. "Come and sit down again."

Tina wished desperately that some other visitors would come along to join them. But there was no one, just the steady hiss of falling rain and now and then a distant rumble of thunder. It was uncomfortable standing around under the low roof, so after a minute or two she did as he bade her. Damn the man! she thought bitterly. He was perfectly well aware of the disturbing effect he had upon her; he delighted in it, arrogantly amused by the sheer male magnetism he exerted so effortlessly.

Tina had to endure another half-hour of torment before the storm abated enough for them to make a dash back to the carpark, and by that time her nerves were at screaming point. Then, instead of driving straight back to Hucclecote Hall, Brant announced that they would go somewhere for lunch, late though it was by now. He took her to an olde-worlde ivy-covered inn near Goodwood House, ancestral home of the Dukes of Richmond and Gordon, driving by way of the by-road that curved around the "Glorious Goodwood" racecourse in its idyllic rural setting. In the oak-beamed restaurant, delicious food was set before them but Tina could scarcely bring herself to touch it. Brant seemed not to notice her agitation. He was too busy expounding on the multitude of facts which his fertile brain had gleaned this morning, while Tina reflected miserably that she herself, a supposed expert in the field, had absorbed precious little from their visit to the open air museum.

She could think of almost nothing now beyond Charles' visit tomorrow, a visit which seemed to loom over her threateningly. Tina administered herself a fierce reprimand. How dreadful to think of the man she loved, the man whom one day she would marry, as a "looming threat."

Should she try to contact Charles by phone? she wondered a little wildly. But what could she say? No, it was a good thing he was coming, she tried to tell herself. This way, she would have the chance to see the two men side by side, be able to compare their true worth. Charles' intelligent conversation and his cultured manners would show Brant Wakefield up for what he was—a man of brashness and crude animality.

So why, she thought despairingly as she went to bed that night, did the prospect of Charles' arrival still fill her with such dread?

Chapter Six

After the rain of the previous day, the Sussex air on Saturday morning was bright and clear. But for Tina the clouds remained, gathering more threateningly with every hour that passed. Charles was due for lunch, and by one o'clock she was on tenterhooks with anxiety.

She had seen nothing of Brant this morning. He was out and about somewhere on the estate, up to his eyes in work, as usual. So she was alone at a window of the Great Hall when she observed the steady progress of a sober black car as it approached along the curving driveway. She crossed through the lobby and went out into the sunshine to stand at the head of the steps.

Charles drew his car to a halt, noticed Tina and raised a hand in smiling salute, then very sensibly reversed so as to leave the car neatly parked and ready to drive off without the need for later maneuvering. Such careful foresight was his invariable habit; but just for once, she thought wistfully, he might have shown a little impetuosity. He might have leapt out to greet her with a fond embrace.

She descended the steps, and had to contain her impatience while Charles reached in the car for his overnight bag, then locked the door and checked the handle. Finally, satisfied that everything was in order, he turned to her.

"Well, Tina my dear, it's nice to see you. Rather sooner than we expected, eh?"

Charles always had an air of gravity—especially cultivated, she half suspected, to gain the awed respect of his students. He was of medium height, a little on the stocky side, with sandy hair and pale brown eyes. Today he was dressed in a lightweight linen jacket and grey trousers . . . his casual togs, as he'd have called them. He was, she knew, two years younger than Brant Wakefield, but looked at least five years Brant's senior.

"Hallo, Charles," she said, injecting a note of warmth into her voice. "It's lovely that you could manage to get away for the weekend."

She tilted up her face and Charles took the hint, touching pursed lips to hers in a gentle peck. It was a kiss that would scarcely have lasted two seconds, yet even so it was cut short. At that precise moment of time Brant Wakefield's voice rang out in greeting as he emerged from the house and hurried down the steps.

"Dr. Medwyn, it's good to see you!" he was exclaiming, his hand outstretched. Then he stopped short in confused apology. "I say, I didn't mean to interrupt anything. I hadn't realised that you and Tina were. . . ."

"How do you do, Mr. Wakefield?" Charles took the proffered hand and nodded smilingly at his host. But there was also a look of discomfort on his squarish face.

"I mean," Brant went on, reverting to his previous remark, "I knew of course that you were Tina's tutor—and her mentor, so to speak. But I had no idea that you two were. . . ." He paused and gave a deprecating little laugh. "Well, for want of a better phrase—in love!"

"We're not. . . ." Tina began hotly, then skidded to an appalled halt. She glanced covertly at Charles, but he seemed not to have been put out by her quick disavowal.

With a certain embarrassment, he said, "Tina and I have known each other for many years, Mr. Wakefield. Since she was a mere child, in fact. Her father, Professor Harcourt, and I were colleagues. More than colleagues, close friends, I am privileged to say."

"I see!" said Brant cheerfully. "Well, do come on in. I'll show you to your room, and then perhaps you'll join us for a glass of sherry before we have lunch?"

"That would be most welcome."

Trailing after the two men, Tina was uncomfortably aware that Brant Wakefield was not at all Charles' sort of person. True, he always respected wealth and high social standing, but there was a rough-hewn quality about Brant which would offend Charles' sensibilities. Not, of course, that he was aware for a single moment of the subtle mockery which lay behind Brant's every word.

Over the luncheon table, Brant expounded admiringly on Tina's qualities.

"Undoubtedly you knew what you were about, Dr. Medwyn, when you selected Tina as the answer to my prayer. I must confess, I wasn't very hopeful when I first wrote to the University. And when I heard that a Miss Clementina Harcourt was coming, I expected some dry-as-dust, middle-aged academic to turn up." He gave Tina a smiling glance across the table . . . a glance that was almost affectionate! "Needless to say, the woman who actually arrived on my doorstep was a delightful surprise. Certainly no one could accuse Tina of being dry as dust." He paused, and added in a softly musing voice that seemed to carry undertones of heaven-knew-what, "Very much the opposite, in fact. Our Tina has proved to be quite a girl!" Another exactly timed pause. "But knowing her intimately as you do, Dr. Medwyn, this can come as no surprise to you."

Charles broke off from the task of easing succulent pieces of flesh from the rainbow trout on his plate. Choosing his words with obvious care, he responded, "Tina is one of the most promising students of her year, and I have every expectation that she will gain a first-class degree. An assignment such as this book of yours, an assignment that calls for flair and initiative, is just what she needs."

"You can say that again!" laughed Brant—an obscurely irreverent remark which earned a reproving frown from Charles, and a nervous scowl from Tina herself. In this mood, she feared, he might come out with anything.

After lunch, Charles and Tina set out together for a stroll around the grounds.

"I can't pretend that I'm exactly enamoured of that fellow Wakefield," he observed. "He's not really . . . well, a gentleman. And he's a jolly sight too casual and flippant about things to my way of thinking."

"Oh, but that's not true," she protested, feeling impelled to defend Brant. "He's doing a wonderful job for the estate, according to Jeff."

"Jeff?" There was a sharpness in Charles' tone, and with a little sigh Tina realised that a certain degree of censorship was called for. Those friendly chats at the farmhouse over tea, that visit to the cheerful village pub, were things best left unmentioned.

"Jeff Lintott is the estate bailiff," she explained. "We've stopped for a chat once or twice, when our paths have happened to cross."

They had reached the lake and stood on the grassy bank, looking across the stretch of sunlit water. At once a pair of swans veered in their direction, hoping for tidbits. The noble birds mated for life, Tina remembered, faithful until death, and one pined away of a broken heart if the other died. Would Charles have any understanding of such loving devotion? she wondered wistfully.

"I have to say frankly, my dear Tina," he began, his hand impatiently smoothing down the sandy hair which had been slightly ruffled by the wind, "that I am not altogether happy about the arrangements here."

"What on earth do you mean, Charles?" she asked wonderingly.

Frowning, he looked down at the grass on which they stood, scoring a line with the toe of his well-polished Oxford brogue.

"I had supposed there would be more people around . . . in the household, I mean. I'm not sure that it's quite the thing, Tina, you being alone in that upstairs apartment with a man like Wakefield."

"I'm not alōne," she protested, altogether too quickly. "There's Mrs. Moncrieff, the housekeeper. She lives in."

Charles conceded this point with a brief shrug of his shoulders. Clearly, he thought it irrelevant. "From the remarks Wakefield let drop," he went on, "it seems to me that he has led a somewhat rackety sort of life."

"Oh come, Charles," she objected. "Wouldn't you expect a man who's made his own way in the world, ending up with the ownership of a huge sheep station in New South Wales, to be something of a rough diamond?"

"*Rough diamond?*" he ejaculated, jerking round to face her. "The use of that phrase implies approbation. An incorrect usage of the English language has never been one of your faults, Tina, so am I to take it that you hold the man in high esteem?"

Colour raged to her cheeks, and to hide it she turned back to the swans, stooping and snapping encouraging fingers at them. But with no offering of food forthcoming, they slid away in stately disgust.

"I only meant," she said, her voice sounding husky, "that he seems to have the right ideas about Hucclecote Hall. His predecessor, Sebastian Wakefield, had let the estate run down badly, and if his son Richard had inherited it things would have rapidly gone from bad to worse. I'm not suggesting," she added, daring to face Charles again now, "that it was a good thing the poor chap was killed in a car crash. But the fact remains that he was, and nothing anyone can do will bring him back. So it's turned out lucky that the next in line is a man of Brant Wakefield's calibre."

An anxious look appeared on Charles' face. "I suppose it's only natural that at your age you should be highly impressionable," he said, in gentle admonition. "But there is a big difference, Tina, between admiring a man for his better qualities, and going overboard in totally uncritical adulation."

What more could she say, Tina wondered in dismay, without digging an even deeper pit for herself? So she remained silent.

Charles, eyeing her flushed cheeks askance, went on thoughtfully, "It might be better all around, you know, for you to find yourself a room in an hotel nearby. With your little car it would be easy for you to get here each day."

"Charles, you can't be serious," Tina cried, appalled. "How on earth would I explain it? What would Mr. Wakefield think of me?"

"You're here to do a particular job of work," he pointed out sharply, his patience fraying. "And by all accounts you've made a first-class start on it. Whether you choose to live here or at an hotel is really no concern of Mr. Wakefield's."

With a feeling of desperation, Tina knew she had to

oppose this suggestion. To move out would be an admission that she was afraid . . . not so much of Brant, but of *herself,* of her own unstable emotions. She could envision the mockery that would gleam in those slate-grey eyes of his at the news that she was moving to a hotel. Besides, in her own mind she admitted that she didn't want to quit her charming room at Hucclecote Hall, with its view over undulating grounds to the lake and the gentle folds of the South Downs.

Anxiety made her voice shrill as she protested, "Honestly Charles, you haven't much faith in me, have you? Or are you seriously imagining that Brant Wakefield is going to come to my room one night and try to rape me?"

A look of severe distaste flitted across Charles' face, "Really, Tina, must you use such a crude expression?" His critical glance probed her. "I imagine you have a lock on your door, and that you make use of it?"

"Of course!" she lied, as the easiest way out. She couldn't possibly explain that there wasn't the smallest need for such a precaution—not after those hateful words Brant had gritted out the night he climbed up to her balcony. *Once I'm gone, you'll have no need to lock your door against me. Not tonight or any other night. You'll be left to enjoy your maidenly peace.*

Somehow, she summoned up a brisk, matter-of-fact voice. "Charles, you're only here until tomorrow morning, so hadn't we better make full use of what little time we have together by going through the preliminary work I've done? I'd be grateful for your help on several points that I've found a bit confusing. You'll no doubt solve in minutes things that would take me a whole day or more to puzzle out."

He smiled at her benignly, taking her hand and pressing it within his larger one. "I'm foolish to worry about you, Tina my dear. I ought to know that with your upbringing you can be relied upon to act level-headedly. You're quite right, of course . . . Wakefield's character is of no importance; it's your research here that matters. We are wasting valuable time talking about him when we have far more relevant things to discuss."

Would Brant, she wondered, show such a blind faith in Loretta Boyd-French, the women *he* intended to marry? Would he be so easily persuaded that she was completely unsusceptible to the proximity of another man? Tina closed her eyes against an inner pain as she and Charles began to walk purposefully towards the house.

The moon, riding silently in the midnight sky, cast a wedge of silver light across Tina's bed. For ages, ever since retiring early, she had been lying awake tossing and turning restlessly. Now the serene beauty of the night drew her to her window.

There was a welcome coolness in the air since yesterday's rain. But even so, Tina felt suffocated in the great, silent house. Within the upstairs apartment—in the rooms on either side of her, in fact—the two men who were causing her so much heartache lay sleeping. She felt caught in a trap between them, and longed to be at a safe distance where she could begin to think clearly.

On a sudden impulse she slipped into her lightweight nylon robe, then made her way down from the apartment by the route she had used once before, the outside steps from the drawing room balcony. She wore no slippers, wanting to enjoy again that delicious, almost voluptuous feeling of walking barefoot across the dewy grass.

On this side of the house everything was in dense

shadow. Tina felt her way along the paved terrace to
the corner, then paused with a gasp of delight. Two
hundred yards away on its knoll, the little Grecian
temple glowed palely in the moon's radiance, a circle of
Doric columns surmounted by a pretty, round dome. In
daylight it had never looked quite so beautiful, the
exactness of its symmetry quite so perfect. She felt
drawn to it irresistibly. There, surely, she would find
peace of mind for a brief while?

She mounted the half dozen stone steps and passed
between two of the columns, which threw bars of black
shadow across the flagstones. Facing her was the stout
carved door set in a grandiose portal. She expected to
find it locked, but it yielded to the pressure of her
fingers, swinging open silently.

Inside, it took a minute or two before her eyes
became accustomed to the moonlight filtering from the
ring of circular windows set high in the wall beneath the
dome. To her surprise, the little round room appeared
to be furnished . . . a couple of wickerwork lounger
chairs, a low table, and what looked like a divan bed.
Wondering, she stretched out her hand and felt soft
springing give to her touch.

Tina jerked upright and swung round at a low
chuckle from the doorway. The tall, broad-shouldered
figure of Brant Wakefield was silhouetted against the
outer moonglow.

"You . . . !" she gasped. "But . . . but how did you
know that I was here?"

"These seductive midsummer nights seem to affect
us in the same way," he said lazily. "I couldn't sleep,
either. I was having a quiet stroll on the terrace when I
saw you coming down the steps from the house."

"You followed me here?"

"You were moving so purposefully, I wanted to find

out why," he explained. "What's the sudden attraction of the temple?"

He took a step inside, and instinctively Tina retreated against the wall. He was wearing, as far as she could discern in the diffused glimmer of light in here, a short silk dressing robe and nothing else. Like herself, he was barefoot.

"It . . . it looked so pretty in the moonlight," she faltered. "And then I found that the door was unlocked. I was just wondering why it was furnished." Her voice gathered assurance as she enlarged upon a theme that would keep more dangerous topics at bay. "I know it was built as a sort of folly by one of the Wakefields at the end of the eighteenth century, but I didn't realise that there was a proper room inside."

Brant chuckled. "A very useful room, too, from what I gather! My cousin Richard used it as a trysting place when he entertained his various girlfriends. As you can see, he had it fitted up with all the . . . shall we say amenities?"

Tina knew that she ought not to remain here a moment longer. Her heart thudded at the thought of the dreadful risk she was exposing herself to, alone with Brant Wakefield in the secret stillness of the summer night, only half dressed and infinitely vulnerable. She knew from past experience how swiftly his verbal taunts could change to surging passion . . . the scornful passion of kisses that inflamed her whole being with yearning, exposing her deeply hidden wanton nature.

She took a deep, steadying breath, then moved to pass him swiftly and sweep out through the open door. But his vicelike grip closed around her wrist and she was jerked back. To her dismay Tina heard the heavy door thud shut, heard, to her deepening horror, the grating of a key being turned in the lock.

"You are not going yet, Clementina," he drawled. "You and I have some talking to do."

"Talking?" Her voice came as a frightened whisper. "What . . . what about?"

"Your relationship with Charles Medwyn," he returned grimly. "If what passes between you two can be graced with the term relationship!" The fingers at her wrist tightened into a torturing manacle of steel. "From various things you let drop about him, I had formed the opinion that the man didn't amount to much. But I never dreamt he would turn out to be quite such a cold fish."

Tina tugged and twisted impotently to escape his grasp. But it was obvious that she would only be free when he chose to release her, and not before.

"I'm not going to stay here and listen to you insulting Charles," she cried.

"You haven't much choice, sweetheart," he informed her, "because I'm going to be doing quite a lot of that! Good grief . . . that kiss of greeting he gave you when he arrived here! It was about as exciting as a peck from a pet parakeet."

"Just because Charles doesn't happen to make a display of his emotions," she began hotly, "it doesn't mean. . . ."

"Has he got any emotions to make a display *of?*" Brant sneered.

"Charles doesn't automatically lust after every passable female he encounters," she flung back.

"Do you think he has ever lusted after *any* woman? Even you, my dear Tina, with your eminently desirable body?" Brant paused enquiringly, then seemed to take her silence as sufficient answer. "He's what . . . over thirty?"

"He's thirty-two, if it's any concern of yours."

"And from what I gathered tonight over the dinner table, there are vague plans in the air of wedding bells when you get your M.A. and he gets his professorship." Brant's voice sounded wrathful. "What sort of pallid blood runs in the man's veins, that he can contemplate waiting that long?"

"Charles loves me," Tina muttered, with a pathetic attempt at dignity.

"Oh yes . . . I was wondering when that much overused word was going to crop up," he barked scathingly. "It seems to me that 'love' is used as an excuse to cover a multitude of sins . . . sins of omission! Okay, so desire can occur without love—I ought to know that, if anyone does! But when loves does exist, then desire has got to play an important part if that love is to have any real meaning."

"Are you describing what you feel for Loretta?" she asked, wondering a little at her own temerity.

"Leave Loretta out of this!" he snapped.

"Gladly," she retorted, "and Charles too, if you don't mind."

"Agreed!" In the dimness Tina saw a glint in the shadowed recesses of his eyes. "So, then—it's down to just you and me."

"No," Tina exclaimed, shrinking from him. "I didn't mean that."

"Why not? Aren't you interested in hearing what I think of you?"

She shouldn't have hesitated, not even for a split second, before saying, "No, of course I'm not!"

"Liar!" he said softly. "What woman doesn't want to hear a man's opinion of her?"

"A *decent* man's opinion, perhaps," Tina protested wildly.

His voice was softer still, a rasp deep in his throat.

"The sort of men you would term 'decent' are for the Clementinas of this world. Not for the warm-blooded, responsive woman who is the real you."

Tina made a frantic effort to inject a scornful worldliness into her voice. "Aren't you making mountains out of a couple of stolen kisses?" she threw out. "I thought you'd been around, Mr. Wakefield!"

He jerked her closer so that their faces were almost touching, and she could feel his warm breath against her cheek.

"Yes, I've been around!" he gritted. "Enough to recognise you for what you truly are. I'll tell you this, my sweet and puritanical little Clementina . . . if you were to give your Charles the least hint of the time-bomb he's planning to take for his wife, the man would turn tail and run from sheer terror."

Tina *had* to fight back. Not to do so would be admitting the truth of his abominable charge against her.

"So I responded to a certain extent when you kissed me . . . is that so very terrible?" she asked, with a forced little laugh. "But if you imagine it was anything more than the lightest flirtation, why do you suppose I immediately sent you packing each time?"

"Advance and retreat," Brant sneered. "The age-old weapon of your sex! Every woman knows that forbidden fruit tastes sweetest to a man. Oh, I don't deny it was a very effective ploy. In those moments I was wild to have you. I wanted you as much—*more,* I'll confess it—as I have ever wanted any woman before . . ."

Tina caught her breath as he paused, her heart thudding in painful beats. "Do you wonder why I didn't take what I wanted?" he queried bitterly. "I'll tell you why, Tina Harcourt. It's because I demand something else from a woman besides a lovely face and a beautiful body. Something that goes beyond the mere gratification of the senses."

"You mean . . . love?" she whispered. "But you have denied love, Brant . . . spurned it."

He said impatiently, "Perhaps love is attainable for the fortunate few—I don't know. What I'm talking about is honesty, the ability to face the truth about oneself, about one's basic nature. You are a deeply sensuous woman, Tina, whose body cries out for fulfilment. Yet you try to pretend you're a prim and proper little maiden from some Victorian parsonage. If you marry Charles Medwyn, you'll spend long years in torment and frustration. And that's why I won't allow it to happen. He wouldn't be happy, either, and you would be throwing your life away."

Even now she flung up defenses against the truth that Brant was thrusting at her so ruthlessly. How, in her secret heart, could she deny a single word of what he said? And yet she *must*. If there was to be any hope of salvation for her, she had to be constantly on guard—all her lifetime through—against the dark side of her nature which threatened to destroy her.

"I shall marry Charles," she said defiantly. "There is no possible way you can stop me."

Brant let go his hold on her wrist so suddenly that she felt, not miraculously free, but oddly bereft. She stood rubbing the bruised and tender flesh, unaware of any pain, but only of the remembered feel of his fingers.

"I can stop you, Tina, and I will," he threatened quietly. "Unless and until you give me your solemn word that you will *not* marry Charles Medwyn, you will remain locked in here with me. For the rest of the night, if necessary."

"You can't keep me here," she gasped. "Suppose . . . suppose I shout for help?"

"By all means do so," Brant returned. "If anyone should happen to hear you, which I doubt, I'll be most interested in the explanation you offer them for your present plight."

She was silent. After a while, he asked, "So which is it to be, Tina? Your promise—or incarceration?"

"I'll never make you that promise!" she hissed passionately.

"Then there's no more to be said! I suggest we try to get some sleep."

In the filtered moonlight, Tina glanced around her desperately. The door was locked and the key was in the pocket of Brant's robe. The circle of windows was high overhead, far out of reach. With fear in her heart, she watched him stretch his lean length on one of the wickerwork loungers.

"You may take the couch," he told her politely. "You needn't worry, I shan't molest you—much as I am tempted." He laughed suddenly, without a trace of humour. "Just think, my dear, if I were to let you have your way and go ahead with your plan to marry Charles Medwyn, this would be the nearest you'd ever get to spending a night with a real man."

"You call yourself a man!" she charged with bitter scorn. "You're nothing but a bullying lout."

"Now then, Blue Eyes!" he chided. "If you're not very careful I shall put you across my knee and spank you like a naughty little girl. But then again, perhaps that's just what you're hoping I'll do."

There was a ring in his voice that warned Tina he was quite capable of carrying out his threat. So she choked back words of protest and stood shivering, hands clasping bare arms, suddenly conscious of a chill in the night air. After a while, she fumbled her way to the couch and found a folded rug there. Wrapping it round her, she curled up as far from him as possible, though she made sure that she could still watch him carefully. At least eight or nine feet separated them, but it might have been no more than eight or nine inches judging from her intense awareness of his proximity. From where she lay huddled his eyes were pools of dark shadow. Were they closed, or was he watching her just as she was watching him?

With the slowly-stealing passage of time the shafts of moonlight moved imperceptibly across the mosaic floor. Gradually, Tina's eyelids drooped, fluttered open, then drooped again. The last thing to linger in her consciousness was the steady sound of Brant's breathing. She was fast asleep when he rose stealthily, careful not to let the wicker chair creak, and came to tuck the rug more securely round her slender form. In Tina's dream, he bent and gently touched his lips to her silky hair.

Chapter Seven

Tina opened her eyes to strange surroundings and wondered where she was. Then instant awareness crashed down on her and she shuddered with dismay. The bright morning sunlight was slanting through one of the high circular windows directly onto her face, dazzling her so that she couldn't see. Moving her head slightly, she found herself confronted by Brant's sardonic gaze.

"You had a good sleep," he observed drily.

He was standing only a yard away from her, his teak-brown hair ruffled, an unshaven shadow darkening his jaw. His short robe, of black silk with crimson facings, was tied loosely at the waist, revealing an expanse of suntanned chest with its haze of dark hair, and the hard muscles of his thighs and calves gleamed a rich bronze.

Hastily, Tina drew the rug closer about her, and up to the chin. "What's the time?" she asked anxiously.

Brant glanced at the wide gold bank around his wrist. "Ten to nine!"

"Oh no!" she gasped in horror. "Charles will be wondering where we are."

"Doubtless!"

Her blue eyes accused him scornfully. "This is what you wanted to happen, isn't it?"

Charles had been insistent, at dinner last night, about wanting to make an early start back this morning—by nine at the very latest, he'd said. He had left his team encamped in one of the Midland towns, but was joining up with them again at a mining centre a hundred miles further north. "I need to be there in time to formulate our plans for Monday," he'd explained.

"Kindly open the door at once," Tina muttered savagely through tight lips, as she scrambled to her feet.

"What makes you think it's locked?" Brant enquired.

So this was the sound that had wakened her just now—the key being turned. The locked door had served its purpose! Tina felt mortified to realise that she had made things easy for Brant by dropping off to sleep while she was his prisoner. How could she possibly explain this to Charles?

I'd better not even try, she decided, as she hurried out into the sunshine and fled down the steps and across the dewy grass which, this morning, no longer gave her a delicious tingling between her toes, but only an unpleasant feeling of chill. She was distressingly aware that Brant was following close on her heels.

Rounding the corner of the house, Tina halted in consternation. Charles was standing on the drawing room balcony, hands resting on the balustrade, staring down at her in horrified disbelief—at her and at Brant! She wished desperately that she could turn tail and run . . . run for ever and ever from the ghastly confrontation that she knew was ahead of her.

She realised that Brant had stopped too, and was standing right behind her. She felt him grip her shoulder . . . could he be giving her courage? No, it was a display for Charles' benefit, compounding the heinous offence she had committed.

"He's not worth being afraid of," he jeered, whispering into her left ear. "Go on, get it over with!"

She tore herself away from the fingers that were moulded to her shoulder, and threw Brant a glance which carried a whole range of emotions . . . anger, shame, and a desperate plea for his pity—that he should spare her from any further humiliation.

Wretchedly, she gathered her flimsy robe about her, aware that in the brilliant light of morning it must make her look flauntingly immodest, and made her way up the stairway. Charles waited in tight-lipped silence until she had gained the balcony, with Brant only a step or two behind her.

"I think," Charles informed her coldly in his most censorious voice, "that I am owed an explanation."

Without any real hope, Tina launched into one that he might just possibly accept. "Oh Charles, I'm most terribly sorry to have made you late in getting away," she prattled. "The point is, Mr. Wakefield and I both woke early . . . it was so terribly hot and stuffy in the night, wasn't it? We were each of us strolling in the grounds to get some fresh air and we came across one another . . . and we sort of got talking and forgot about the time."

Stark disbelief burned in Charles' eyes. Yet would he be any readier to believe the actual truth, Tina wondered in despair, even supposing she could bring herself to tell him?

Brant put in cheerfully, "We'd better go and get dressed, Tina, hadn't we? It's unfair of us to keep Dr. Medwyn hanging around any longer for his breakfast."

Charles' normally placid face was well-nigh apoplectic, his pale brown eyes bulging from their sockets.

"If you imagine that I'd touch so much as another morsel in your house, Wakefield, you are grossly mistaken. Now, if you please, I would like a word alone with . . . with Miss Harcourt.''

Brant said easily, "I think I'd better hang around, just to see fair play."

But Tina had seen the almost maniacal glint in Charles' eyes, and she didn't want Brant to overhear what he might say to her if his tightly-controlled temper snapped completely and he took to verbal abuse. She touched Brant's arm timidly. "Please!" she beseeched him, "leave us alone for a few minutes."

He hesitated a moment, his eyes flashing a dangerous warning to Charles that made the other man turn pale, then said to Tina, "Very well, I'll leave you—if you're sure that's what you want." He crossed the drawing room at an unhurried pace and left through the door.

Charles began, each syllable heavy with distaste, "I never imagined I should live to see such a day, Tina. And you so blatant about your carryings on . . . strolling back to the house with your lover in broad daylight as if you have nothing of which to be ashamed."

"He is not my lover," she said doggedly.

Charles crossed to the marble fireplace, standing with his back to it, hands clasped behind him, like some stern Victorian paterfamilias.

"There is no sense in making things worse by lying to me, Tina. You come back from a night of wantonness, blear-eyed with your hair all rumpled—him too!—and both of you with hardly a stitch of clothing on! I had imagined," he went on with cold fury, "that any such flaw in your nature had been eradicated by your careful upbringing. By the wise guidance of your father and the steadying influence of your aunt. But alas, all their efforts have been to no avail, the evil is too deeply embedded. It is a case of like mother, like daughter!"

"You . . . you're being unfair," she stammered in a whisper.

"Am I, Tina? Your mother was married to one of the finest men I have ever had the honour to know. An eminent and highly respected academic. Anyone would suppose that her cup of happiness was brimming over. She moved in the most exalted circles, and she had a gracious and extremely comfortable home in the University precincts. She also had an infant daughter to care for—you. Yet even with all this she could not keep a bridle on her lustful instincts, but allowed them to lead her into a sordid *affaire*."

Tina closed her eyes against the pain of this barrage. She could recall her mother as only the most shadowy figure . . . in wistful memory a soft and loving person who had cradled her little daughter and soothed her hurts with gentle kisses, who used to sing her to sleep with a dreamy lullaby. But undeniably, there had been a different side to Deidre Harcourt's nature. Undeniably, she had met her death with her lover late one night in his car. Aunt Ruth, hastening down from Northumberland to take over her brother's household and care for his three-year-old motherless daughter, had seen to it that Tina knew the truth. Over the years of her growing up the vague allusions and hints had become more specific until every squalid detail was laid bare for her—as a salutary warning!

"She'd been carrying on with that wretched man for ages," her spinster aunt had spat out disgustedly, "and your poor dear father was far too trusting ever to suspect anything. The scandal broke poor Ernest's heart—not to mention nearly ruining his career."

And behind Aunt Ruth's every word on the subject lay the suggestion that Tina must inevitably be tarred with the same brush as her mother. That bad blood would declare itself unless she kept herself under rigorous control. In the child's upbringing, emphasis had been laid on the loftier aspects of life, the things of the intellect and the spirit. And when, in her teens, Tina had sensed the first stirrings of something more primitive in her nature, she had been terrified. And never had she let herself go beyond the occasional tussle with an amorous fellow-student who, because of her special relationship with Dr. Medwyn, hadn't dared to press for much more than a goodnight kiss. And even these innocuous encounters had left Tina riddled with shame and remorse until she had somehow reasoned herself into accepting them as only the normal, high-spirited indulgence of young people.

Charles Medwyn represented everything that was safe and solid and decent in the world. Approved of by her father and her aunt, he would provide her with the sort of background in which she would eventually find the fulfilment proper in a nice young woman while those other, wayward impulses, which Charles had never even fleetingly aroused, could be repressed and finally eliminated. Tina had earnestly cherished this fond hope until Brant Wakefield exploded into her life, his kisses awakening blatant desires that shocked her with their intensity. She hated him, loathed him, for ripping aside the mantle of respectability in which she had so carefully clothed herself till now.

Tina's thoughts spun in a jostling tumult. If she were to leave Hucclecote Hall today with Charles, abandon the project of her book, could she escape from the surging current that was threatening to sweep her to destruction? She could . . . she must!

But even as she turned to Charles beseechingly, he was saying in a curt, clipped tone, "I don't think there is any point in our discussing this distasteful business any longer, Tina. It is fortunate—for us both, I believe—that I came here this weekend and found you out in time."

"You mean . . . ?" she whispered, her mouth dry.

"Whatever the understanding there might have been between us, it must now be regarded as at an end," he elucidated. "I shall leave here immediately, and I suggest that we do not maintain contact. When you return to University in the autumn, I shall arrange for you to be transferred to the supervision of another tutor."

Tina opened her mouth to protest, but the words stuck in her throat. She refused to beg for Charles' mercy. If he truly thought so badly of her—perhaps had just cause for thinking so badly of her—there could never be any chance of happiness for them together.

In the dark pit of her depression, was there perhaps the faintest glimmer of relief? Yet how could she possibly feel relief at the prospect of losing her secure protection against her own tainted nature?

From somewhere she found the dignity to say, "Very well, Charles. If that's how you feel, then so be it!"

His pale brown eyes widened with astonishment. "You're not even going to try and deny anything?" he queried.

"What would be the point?" she shrugged. From whence had she suddenly gained this amazing feeling of poise, this head-high sense of confidence? "I'm going to get dressed now, Charles, and I expect that you'll be gone before I return. So I'll say goodbye!"

Tina walked to the door quite steadily, and was thankful to find the corridor empty. But once in the privacy of her room, her movements became jerky, uncoordinated. Going through to the adjoining bathroom, she turned on a gushing stream of hot water. She let her robe drop and slipped out of her flimsy nightdress. The full-length mirror on the bathroom wall offered a reflection of her naked body, the treacherous body that could bring about her downfall. On one shoulder lingered a purplish bruise from the brutal imprint of Brant's thumb. Tina gave a little shiver. As the bath filled, so the mirror became steamed over, her reflection slowly fading until there was only an impenetrable mist.

Chapter Eight

For three days after Charles' abrupt departure, Tina barely so much as caught sight of Brant. Nor did she want to. It was bad enough having to live with her misery, without having him present to relish it, his dark eyes sardonic and taunting.

At mealtimes he pointedly kept out of her way, eating at odd hours or not at all, greatly to Mrs. Moncrieff's concern.

"There's this lovely roast duckling," she complained to Tina, "from Jeff's own farmyard, and done nicely to a turn—though I say so myself! It's a wicked waste, lassie, for you canna eat it all. And the master having just bread and cheese at the village pub for his lunch, I dinna doubt."

Tina ate a little of the breast meat and a spoonful of vegetables, but with small appetite. When the housekeeper returned with a dish of rhubarb fool for dessert she also brought with her a folded newspaper and a barely suppressed air of excitement.

"Well now, who'd have thought it?" she began, putting down the cut crystal bowl with unwonted cluminess. "Mind you, it's for the best, to my way of thinking. He's had a narrow escape, if you ask my opinion."

Puzzled, Tina enquired what she was talking about,

and had the newspaper thrust under her nose. Mrs. Moncrieff stabbed a thin finger at a column headed, *Cabaret star to wed for third time*. As Tina began to read, a tremor ran the length of her spine. In typical journalese, it related that an engagement had just been announced between Chuck Flanders, international singing star, and the Hon. Loretta Boyd-French, only daughter of Viscount Boyd-French of Maddehurst Manor. The marriage would take place hurriedly before the couple left for Chuck's new season at a nightclub in Las Vegas. It would be recalled, the report went on, that Chuck Flanders' divorce from blues singer Angie Walters was made absolute only a week ago. This announcement scotched the rumours, it concluded, of a romance between the Hon. Loretta and the new heir to the Hucclecote Hall estate, Mr. Brant Wakefield, to whose cousin, the late Mr. Richard Wakefield, she had formally been engaged before his untimely death last year in a car crash.

Tina looked up, heart pounding, and met the house-keeper's frowning gaze.

"I never liked her, you know," Mrs. Moncrieff confided. "Though mind you, she'd have done well enough for Mr. Richard . . . they were two of a kind. But not for Mr. Brant. He's an entirely different kettle of fish."

Tina nodded weakly, unable to summon up any suitable comment. Mrs. Moncrieff was far from inhibited, though, and gossiped on, "I've been wondering what's been upsetting the master lately. Ever since he came back from London he's been a bit strange, and these last three days . . . well, he's been in a mood to snap your head off for the smallest thing. That's not a bit like him, but I suppose it's understandable if he's been jilted. A thing like this is bound to be a blow to a man's pride, whoever he is."

After her skimpy lunch, Tina returned to the library. But she found herself even less able to focus her attention on work. She was making so little progress, she acknowledged to herself with a sigh, that she would seriously have to consider admitting defeat and quitting the project.

To her great astonishment, Brant joined her for dinner that evening, entering the dining salon at the last moment just as she was sitting down. His dark eyes gleamed in the glow of the setting sun, but his craggy face was a blank mask, totally unreadable.

"Would you care for a glass of sherry before we eat, Tina?" he enquired politely.

"No, thank you," she replied in a low voice.

He shrugged his indifference, and poured a whisky for himself. Mrs. Moncrieff came in just then with a tureen of chilled consommé, and her eyes lit up at the sight of him.

"Oh, I'm so glad you decided to be in this evening, Mr. Wakefield," she exclaimed. "There's plenty for you, of course . . . I always do plenty."

"Fine!" he said, uncaring.

"Mind you," the housekeeper ventured, "I wasn't really expecting to see you here for dinner, not after reading in the paper. . . ."

"That will be all, Mrs. Moncrieff," he clipped, slate eyes hardening to steel.

The housekeeper knew better than to utter another word, and instantly withdrew. There was a ponderous silence in the room. Brant was standing behind Tina's chair now, and she could feel the pressure of his gaze on the back of her head.

"Well," he enquired calmly, "aren't you going to serve the soup?"

"If you're ready."

"I'd hate to delay you," he returned, coming into

view and taking the chair at the place which was invariably laid for him, whether he was at home or not.

Tina found it difficult to spoon the soup to her mouth while her hands were trembling so. After a few moments, Brant observed drily, "I don't doubt there has been some cosy speculation between you and my highly-treasured, if rather loquacious, housekeeper!"

Tina made no attempt to refute this statement.

"In that delightful Scottish brogue of hers," he went on, "I detected a note of righteous indignation on my behalf. Is that an opinion which you share, Miss Harcourt? Or would vindictive pleasure be a more apt description in your case?"

She tried to still the shaking soup spoon. "Why should you imagine I care at all?" she said evenly.

Dark eyes narrowed, lancing into her. "So you admit that you know what I'm talking about?"

"I could scarcely not know. You *are* newsworthy, Mr. Wakefield."

His broad shoulders eased into a shrug. "In the gutter press, perhaps—they go for anything that provides a spicy bit of sensationalism. Not that there's much mileage for them in this case. Now if Loretta and I had already been married and she had run off with him . . . that would have given them something to blazon in lurid headlines." He shot her a harsh, challenging look. "Do you approve of Loretta's action?"

"I neither approve nor disapprove," Tina tossed back.

"Oh, but I think you do! I think that inside that pretty little head of yours, you're gloating! Well, here's something more for you to gloat about. Loretta told me, if you please, that I bore her stiff with my dedicated resolve to make the Hucclecote Hall estate pay its way. She said that, as I had plenty of money coming in from my sheep station in Australia, it was just a stupid waste of time and effort, and she wanted a life that offered more excitement." His voice became charged with anger. "The sort of cheap excitement, presumably, that she'll get drifting around the world with that drunken wastrel, Flanders. I wish her joy of him, and him of her!"

The thought that had been swelling in Tina's brain found voice now in bitter denunciation.

"So this explains your disgusting behaviour on Saturday night!" she cried. "You arrive back here after quarrelling with Loretta in London, with all your plans in ruins, so you decided—out of sheer dog-in-the-manger spite—that you'd ruin my life with Charles! You couldn't bear the thought of other people being happy, just because you weren't even capable of making a marriage of convenience!"

If the width of the dinner table had not been dividing them, Tina imagined that Brant would have struck her. His eyes blazed, and his voice was husky with the effort of controlling his fury.

"What I did on Saturday night," he ground out, "was not ruin your life, Clementina, but save *you* from ruining it for yourself."

"That's ridiculous," she protested.

"It's not! In your heart, you know it's true."

Across the room the service door opened and Mrs. Moncrieff came in with the Crown Roast of Lamb for the next course, each succulent cutlet prettily embellished with a frilly white collar. Neither of them glanced at her, neither was even aware of her presence, they were too absorbed in the savage intensity of their conflict. As silently as possible the housekeeper withdrew, to put the joint to keep warm in the oven until she was summoned.

The faint click of the closing door seemed to snap a

thread of tension. With a muttered exclamation Brant rose to his feet and strode to the window, standing there staring out across the wooded parkland. Against the westering sun his teak-dark hair glinted with warm colour and, unwillingly, Tina again likened him in her mind to a Greek God—a wrathful God this time, bent on vengeance.

"If you truly believe that losing Charles Medwyn means losing your chance of happiness," he challenged, "why are you still here at Hucclecote Hall? Why aren't you running after the man you're supposed to love so much, begging for his forgiveness and understanding? Surely no degree of self-abasement would be too great a price to pay, if Charles would only consent to take you back? Yet you let him depart and yourself remain here. . . ." Brant's voice changed subtly, back to the hatefully familiar whip-flick of scorn. ". . . here at the scene of the crime, so to speak."

"Charles would never take me back," she murmured tonelessly. "Not after what happened."

"Because of a single transgression?"

The answer to his mocking question screamed at Tina. In Charles' eyes that single transgression had exposed her for what she truly was beneath the thin veneer of respectability—a woman whose physical appetites were well-suited to providing female companionship for a crudely libidinous man like Brant Wakefield.

"Are you saying that you want me to leave here?" she asked, on a thin thread of breath.

"By no means," he clipped. "I see no need for that."

Despairingly, Tina regarded his broad, implacable back. If Brant were to send her packing, that would be a solution to her tormenting problem. But that she herself should find the courage to go away of her own volition . . . it was something else altogether. How could she possibly remain any longer at Hucclecote Hall, though? If she did so, to what new depths of degradation would she have plunged before the summer's end?

Tina's lips parted, and unbidden words emerged. Indeed, she was hardly aware that she was speaking. "Please," she whispered, "what am I to do?"

Through the open French windows the evening breeze rustled the leaves of ancient ivy growing against the wall. A nesting bird chirped sleepily. In the distance, a tractor was making use of the last precious hour of daylight.

Slowly, Brant turned to look at her. His dark eyes, almost black now, pierced her through and held her like a pinned butterfly.

"There is a very simple answer to both our problems, Clementina," he announced. "You had better marry me."

All other sounds were lost in the throbbing of a giant pulse in Tina's head. Seconds fled by, building into minutes. Very slowly, she came out of her daze and anger took over, exploding in a tumult of accusing words.

"How can you stand there and calmly make such an outrageous proposition? It's no wonder that Loretta jilted you, if you treated her with the same sort of contempt. What kind of man are you, that you can casually make use of any woman who happens to be handy? A wife means just one thing to you . . . she merely represents an insurance policy against the loss of your inheritance."

"So!" he murmured softly. "You know about that little clause in the entail, then? As I've had occasion to remark once before, you certainly do your homework, Clementina! But allow me to make a small correction

. . . I'm not asking any woman who happens to be handy. I'm asking *you!*"

"Why me, specially?" she demanded. Then she flung out bitterly, "Oh yes, I understand . . . you've calculated, as Jocelyn Ashley pointed out when he was here, that with my qualifications I'll be useful to have around when you start setting up the craft workshops and things."

Ironic eyebrows quirked. "You also have eminent qualifications in quite another direction, Blue Eyes!"

"Must you always be so hateful?" she stormed.

"I seem to recall one or two occasions," he drawled, "when you found me anything but hateful."

"You're wrong!" she denied passionately, as if vehemence alone would force truth into her words. "What happens in a passing moment doesn't mean a thing. I'm surprised that a man like you reads so much significance into a couple of kisses."

He took two long strides towards her. "They meant nothing to you, those kisses?"

"Nothing!" Tina reiterated.

Two more long strides and he was beside her where she still sat at the dinner table. The familiar grip of steel was on her wrist, jerking her to her feet, knocking the chair aside. His arms closed about her slender figure, moulding it to him as he had done before, and all the remembered pressures of his maleness brought her body to aching awareness. He forced her head back, found her lips and parted them with his hard, bruising mouth. Through her closed eyelids a red mist was enveloping her, threatening her last feeble struggles for self control. She *had* to show him she was right, that her response was of the moment only . . . the instinctive response of female to male that was far from being the clamour of urgent desire that he suggested. To show Brant? No, to show *herself!*"

She was helpless in the iron girdle of his arms, and all protest was stifled by the lips that were pressed so cruelly to hers. Only one course lay open to her. She hesitated a moment longer for the necessary courage, then nipped his lower lip between her teeth. Brant drew back sharply with a cry of mingled surprise and pain.

"So, we have a sharp-toothed vixen!" he murmured ruefully.

"You deserve worse than that!" she breathed, her voice hoarse.

His dark eyes were narrowed, gauging her. "Still pretending you don't like it?" he jeered. "Come now, Miss Tina Harcourt, be honest with yourself for the first time in your life. It would be safe to show your true feelings, once I had made you my wife."

"If I married you," she averred, drawing back from him a step, "I would regret it every single day for the rest of my life."

"But I'd make it my pleasurable duty to see that you didn't regret it," he returned equably. "Come, take a deep breath and consent. I think we'd make an ideal match, don't you? We have such compatability of taste."

"I will not marry you!" she spat.

"You'll forego all the many advantages of being the mistress of Hucclecote Hall? Respected by everyone . . ."

"Respected?" she echoed scornfully.

"Let us say envied, then."

"Huh! No woman who knew you for what you are, Brant Wakefield, would envy me."

"Now there you're making a bad mistake," he jibed. "There's many a woman in Australia, for example, who'd catch the next plane here on receipt of a cabled proposal."

"Then why don't you send one?" she returned, choking.

"Because I'm asking *you*, Clementina."

"You think you could rule me, don't you?" she challenged. "You think you could make me a slave to your whims. But you might find out how wrong you were, if I *did* marry you."

"Try it, and see," he suggested, smiling the smile of a devil.

She took another backward step, to alleviate the intolerable pressure of his nearness. But he came after her, not permitting the smallest degree of escape.

"Say yes, Tina. Just that one little word—yes."

"No!" she sobbed. "I won't, I won't!"

"Say yes," he repeated, with sickening confidence that he would have his way in the end.

Tina found to her amazement that thoughts and arguments for and against were flashing through her brain. The disadvantages were too obvious to dwell upon. But the advantages? An announcement of her engagement to Brant Wakefield would in one stroke refute Charles' cruel denunciation of her . . . for marriage was something he'd never imagine the owner of Hucclecote Hall would contemplate with a woman he regarded as a mere plaything.

As things stood now, the future she had dreamed of lay in ruins. Even if she could find the courage to return to Bellchester in the autumn and boldly continue with her postgraduate studies in the face of Charles' patent disapproval, the outlook for her was bleak indeed. What chance was there of ever making a career for herself in the field of Social History without a good recommendation from the University where she had taken her degree? But here at Hucclecote Hall, as Jocelyn Ashley had suggested, there was work she could usefully do. Work that would be interesting and absorbing, and could bring her a measure of satisfaction.

Moreover, the argument ran on in her mind, to be married to a virile man like Brant would be a just and suitable punishment to her for letting her primitive urges get the upper hand. To deny herself the passion and fulfilment that Brant had it in his power to bring her would be no more than she deserved. And as for Brant himself . . . he would soon discover that his insidious sexuality counted for nothing against her unyielding determination. He would find himself married to a frigid, unresponsive wife. And that, she believed, would be a truly fitting revenge on a man who took such arrogant pride in the sensual power he had over women.

Tina caught her breath in those final fleeting seconds before she sealed her fate. Then she said, with an unnatural calm, "Very well, Brant, I'll marry you."

He looked astounded by her sudden capitulation. "Do you really mean it?" he demanded. "Is that a promise?"

A promise, or a threat? She said coldly, "I said so, didn't I? It's an ominous start, if you intend to question everything I say."

His astonishment lasted for a few more pulsating moments. Then he relaxed and gave a soft laugh deep in his throat.

"Do we seal the bargain with a kiss?"

"No!" she cried, backing away until the sideboard prevented her backing any further. But this time Brant did not pursue her. Instead, he turned on his heel and strode to the door.

"I doubt if either of us wants to finish dinner," he said, pausing a moment, "so I'll leave you now to make your plans. We'll not delay the wedding, I think. Let us say a month from now—the eighteenth."

Then Brant was gone, and she was alone. Had it really happened? Was she committed to spending a lifetime with the man she despised above all others, or was it just a nightmare born in her tortured imagination?

But there on the table were two bowls of consommé, scarcely touched, on the sideboard, the empty whisky glass that Brant had used. And in her mind, the memory of his lips, hard against hers.

Chapter Nine

"What I still fail to understand," Aunt Ruth commented, with a lingering tinge of disapproval in her sharp-
toned voice, "is why the need for such haste?"

She had travelled down to Sussex from her residential hotel in Northumberland to be with Tina for the
week preceding her wedding. A thin, rather gaunt
woman, she tended to view the world through censorious eyes, and was always ready to believe the worst in
any given situation. A letter from her had arrived
within days of Charles' abrupt departure, expressing
horror and disgust at the report of the events he had
lost no time in imparting to her over the telephone.
Accusation screamed from each precisely-penned line
. . . that this was indisputably Tina's mother coming
out in her, the very sort of thing her poor father had
always dreaded. At least it was a mercy that dear
Ernest had not lived to see his daughter's shame and
have his heart broken all over again.

But Tina's own letter to her aunt, announcing her
engagement to the owner of Hucclecote Hall, had
crossed it in the post. This had elicited a second epistle
from Aunt Ruth, very different in tone from the first.
She was impressed, no doubt of that. And any man who
honourably proposed marriage to a girl, for all that he
was coarse and ill-mannered (this was worded most

discreetly) couldn't be wholly condemned. She accepted that in the absence of a Harcourt family home, it
was right and proper for her niece's wedding to take
place in Sussex. The thought of the ceremony being
held in the Wakefields' private chapel added an agree-
able distinction to the proceedings.

All of which did not answer the older woman's
present query as to the need for such unseemly haste.

"Once I had accepted Brant's proposal," Tina said
uneasily, "there seemed no reason for any delay
beyond the calling of the banns."

"But surely . . . even in these impetuous modern
days, an engagement of two or three months would not
be considered unduly long?"

Tina turned away to hide her flushing face, saying,
"Brant didn't want to wait." And she added with
meaningful emphasis, "That's the only reason, Aunt
Ruth."

There was an unmistakable sigh of relief at this
assurance, and Tina could guess what was now passing
through her aunt's mind. Better, perhaps, all things
considered, that the girl should be safely pinned down
in marriage before the unthinkable became a reality.
And a strong man like Brant Wakefield could be relied
upon to keep Tina under firm control and check her
wayward impulses.

For there was no doubt about it, in the two days since
her arrival, Brant had won a high place in Aunt Ruth's
esteem. True, she could often be seen to wince at his
forthright way of putting things. But it was gratifying to
be treated with such deference by the owner of a vast
landed estate with its magnificent ancestral home. And
as a bonus, it appeared to her that he owned nearly half
of Australia! Undeniably, Tina mused, Brant had gone
out of his way to make himself charming to her aunt—a
piece of calculated cynicism on his part, of course!

"I must admit, child, that you seem to have done very well for yourself," Aunt Ruth granted magnanimously, as they two of them strolled in the grounds for a breath of air one sultry afternoon. "Poor Charles was heartbroken, of course . . . and doubtless, in his unhappiness, he exaggerated the situation a little. Mind you, Tina, I won't pretend that I hadn't set my heart on your being the wife of Professor Charles Medwyn. So fitting for your dear father's memory that you should marry a successor of his in the Chair of Social History at Bellchester and return to live in the gracious home in which you were brought up." She squared her thin shoulders bravely, and permitted a trace of wintry indulgence to those who were young and impetuous. "But there it is . . . love must have its way, I suppose!"

Love! That short little word reached Tina, not in Aunt Ruth's sour tones, but with all the harsh mockery of Brant's deep voice.

Since the evening Brant had proposed to her, she had seen little of the man she was supposed to love. She had been alone with him for scarcely an hour at a time . . . for the most part merely over the meal table. These weeks before the wedding had been a strange interlude for her, one in which she had expected to be hectically busy with her preparations. But actually, she had found remarkably little to do. Beyond ordering and attending fittings for her wedding dress, and choosing the rest of her trousseau, the only task which took her any length of time was preparing a list of wedding guests. Brant and Mrs. Moncrieff between them seemed to be attending to everything else, and Tina was content to let them get on with it, telling herself that she didn't care.

It was the subject of money that caused the first argument of their engagement.

"I've opened a bank account in your name," Brant said one day at lunch, tossing a blue-covered cheque-book onto the table. "Buy whatever you want. There's no need to restrict yourself."

"Thank you, but I have my own money," she replied with dignity, grateful for the degree of independence that her father's small inheritance had given her.

Brant shrugged carelessly. "You might as well hang on to your own money. Use mine, there's plenty of it, Lord knows!"

"I'd prefer to use my own," Tina reiterated. "Until we are married, that is."

"And then the spending spree will commence?" he queried lightly.

She coloured, "That's not what I meant."

"No, I know it wasn't," he said, and for once his words were not accompanied by that hateful look of mocking amusement. "All the same, Tina, you might as well get used to the idea of having plenty of money at your disposal."

As the days of her brief engagement went by, Tina came to realise that Brant was not going to demand from her the normal intimate privileges of a fiancé. At first she had been expecting that, at any moment of the day and without warning, he would snatch her into his arms and kiss her passionately. She grew tense with the effort of keeping constantly alert, on guard against permitting the ice in her heart to thaw.

In fact, though, the only kisses he gave her were chaste pecks, administered purely for the sake of appearances . . . a fleeting touch of his lips to hers when they came together in the company of other people. For Aunt Ruth's benefit, for instance, and for the vicar's, at the rehearsal held in the tiny chapel one morning.

Tina discovered that her fiancé had been right in predicting that she would be envied. At the engagement party held at Hucclecote Hall for Brant's friends and various local notables, and at various dinners and cocktail parties to which they were invited, Tina was left in no doubt that she was considered to have won a fantastic prize. Girls of her own age group were uninhibited about speaking their minds, especially when they'd imbibed a few glasses too many of champagne.

One such, a lustrous honey-blond who was the daughter of a local racing-stud owner, drifted over to Tina at the small private dance held one gloriously warm evening on the terrace of her luxurious home.

"You must be feeling just like a cat who's got at the cream," she giggled, steadying herself against one of the supports of a rose arbour. "Honestly, I think Loretta Boyd-French must be out of her tiny mind to chuck a marvellous, sexy hunk of man like Brant Wakefield. And he's positively loaded, too! What more could any girl ask?"

"Talking about me?" It was Brant himself, appearing suddenly from the shadows beyond the patio. On this hot night he wore a white tuxedo, and looked immaculate. Considering how he had been garbed that first time Tina had set eyes on him, it constantly amazed her that he could look so elegant in formal clothes. His manners, too, on occasions such as this, could hardly be faulted.

The blond girl giggled again at Brant's sudden appearance. Abandoning the rose-support, she leaned herself against him instead.

"I was just saying that you're a marvellous, sexy hunk of man," she murmured throatily. Her palms rested against the firm wall of his chest, her long, slender fingernails lightly scratching at the silk of his frilled shirtfront. Brant did nothing to stop her, seeming, in fact, rather to enjoy it, Tina thought.

In the glow of the coloured fairylights strung around the patio, his dark eyes gleamed with devilment. "Are you making me an offer?" he quipped.

The girl gave a quick bubble of laughter from deep in her throat. "Any time, Mr. Gorgeous. You only have to say the word."

"My fiancée might object," he suggested.

Appalled by a savage pang of jealously that left her breathless, Tina strove to sound uncaring. "He's a free agent!" she said with a little laugh. "We don't keep each other on a ball and chain, do we, Brant?"

"Speak for yourself, my sweet," he returned. "Just you try going on the loose, and you'll find that I've got you well and truly hobbled." His tone was one of light raillery, and the other girl would never have discerned the ominous threat behind those words.

From the open French windows of the huge lounge, a stereo was pouring out music for dancing . . . a smooth, sentimental number. Without asking permission, Brant enfolded the other girl in his arms and they began swaying together in rhythm, hardly moving from the spot. Even now he had to taunt her! Sickened, Tina spun away and almost literally swung into the arms of a gratified young man who seized his chance to dance with the most desirable girl at the party. Tina made herself move in sinuous unison with him, snuggling closer and joking with a false flirtatiousness. But she might have been dancing on her own for all she was aware of her partner. The coloured lights became strung together in a single blur, the throbbing music filled her ears. . . .

She felt a piercingly familiar grip of steel on her shoulders, and a lazy voice drawled, "Sorry to break it up, old man. My property, I think."

As Brant was driving her home later, he mentioned that he had concluded a deal for one of the stud's best stallions.

"I've been wanting to get myself a mount with a bit of spirit," he explained. "There are a couple of good mares in the stables back at the Hall for you to choose from, Tina, so we'll be able to go riding together."

"But I don't ride," she protested.

"Then you'll learn," he said flatly. "My wife must ride, as she must perform all the other functions proper to the Lady of Hucclecote Hall, with skill and aplomb."

"You expect too much of me," she muttered.

"Nothing that is beyond your capabilities, Tina," he responded. Another gibe, or a genuine compliment? How would she ever know with this man?

Day by day, the sun had blazed down ever more fiercely. On the morning of the wedding it was stifling in the little chapel, its claustrophobic pews packed with a bigger congregation than it had probably seen for many a year. In their summer dresses the women were much luckier than the menfolk . . . the society guests in full regalia of morning wear, the estate workers togged out in their Sunday best, mopping perspiring foreheads.

A second-cousin of her father's, Uncle Robert, had been summoned from London to give Tina away. On his dignified arm, with her cortège of two diminutive pages and two pretty little dimpled girls—supplied from some distant branch of the Wakefield family—Tina trod the aisle towards the tall figure who stood waiting for her by the altar rail. Jeff Lintott, deeply honoured to be chosen by Brant for his best man, looked almost short beside him, for all his own six feet.

The service began, droned on. Waves of heat shimmered through the pointed stained-glass windows.

Tina performed her part as if by rote, making the correct responses. The ring was slipped on her finger—a manacle as cold as steel. Brant lifted her veil to kiss her, and his lips too felt cold.

After they signed the register in the vestry, the handpumped organ breathed out the Wedding March. With Tina now on her husband's arm, the bridal procession made its way back down the aisle through a sea of faces . . . the many wellwishers smiling and waving, the less well-intentioned observing her through envious eyes. She knew what these latter were thinking . . . it wasn't right or fair that a jumped-up-from-nothing girl should have landed such a fine catch!

Opposite the tiny chapel porch the photographers, (one of them from a London news agency,) waited in the shade of an ancient yew tree. Tina wondered, as if in a dream, what her University friends would make of it when they read in the papers that she had married Brant Wakefield, one of the wealthiest landowners in Sussex. She was thankful that, for the weeks of the long vacation, they were dispersed far and wide, saving her the embarrassment of having her friends present, perhaps seeing through her careful facade.

She and Brant walked back to the house along the path trodden by Wakefields through the centuries, and the village children skipped along beside them. Brant invited each and every one of them to partake of the special spread set out on long tables in the conservatory.

The reception proper was held in the Great Hall, where the air was heady with the scent of massed roses. Tina stood beside Brant to receive their guests, her face set in a forced smile. Her somewhat bewildered state was attributed to the extreme heat. It was trying for them all, everyone agreed, but especially so for the bride. Only Brant looked cool. "I've known it thirty degrees higher than this in Australia," he laughingly explained to those who commented.

The caterers' men served the buffet wedding breakfast, while Mrs. Moncrieff, a guest today, watched the arrangements with needle-sharp eyes. There were various speeches that Tina hardly even heard, an endless round of greetings, the four-tiered cake to be cut. She and Brant posed together with the silver knife held at the ready, his large hand clasping hers, so that the agency man could capture the moment.

"How do you feel about getting married, Mr. Wakefield?" he demanded. "Will you give me a quote, please?"

Brant's smiling, handsome face was turned to his bride as he replied, the dark eyes sparking a challenge.

"Let me see now . . . you can quote me as saying, 'With little hope of ever achieving my ambition, I shall do my utmost to be the husband that Tina deserves.'"

There was an outburst of applause from the guests at his nicely-turned phrase which conveyed such considerate devotion. But as Tina slipped upstairs to change, she carried in her heart the overtones of mockery which only she could understand.

Chapter Ten

Aunt Ruth, glowing with pride at the undoubted success of the wedding festivities, fussed around Tina as she slipped out of her bridal gown and donned her going-away outfit. A dress and short-fitting jacket in hyacinth blue silk, it softly emphasised the slender curves of her body and enhanced her creamy complexion and the deeper blue of her eyes.

Downstairs again, there were a hundred goodbyes to be said, and a snowstorm of confetti to be run through before Jeff drove the happy couple away in Brant's white Mercedes, en route to the airport. A week in Paris was to be their honeymoon. There was too much needing Brant's attention at the moment for more than that, too many contracts in the process of being negotiated.

"We'll take longer away in the winter," he promised her, as the car purred along the country road between flower-starred verges that, at this time of the year, were a symphony of purples and mauves. "I shall need to spend a few weeks or so in Australia then. You'll like it there."

The winter? Did so far ahead in time have any real meaning? Tina could barely envisage even the next few hours.

It was as hot in Paris as in Sussex. But the luxury hotel close to the Place de la Concorde was air-

conditioned. The bridal suite was on the second floor, a
large sitting room and an equally large bedroom, both
lavishly furnished in the ornate style of Louis the
Fifteenth.

"How about a stroll along the Champs Élysées, and a
glass of wine at a pavement cafe before dinner?" Brant
suggested. "Just to get the flavour of Paris."

"I'm tired," Tina protested dispiritedly.

"We can't have that on our wedding night," he threw
back, his eyes amused. "Lie down and rest for an hour,
then, while I go out on my own."

When he had departed, Tina stood at the tall window
of the luxurious room, gazing out at the graciously-
balconied buildings opposite and the trees of the
nearby park. She kicked off her shoes and stood in
stockinged feet, enjoying the softness of the thick-pile
carpet. Ten minutes later, having removed her jacket
and dress and slipped into a satin robe, she was
surprised by a tap on the door. It proved to be a waiter
with a tray of tea ordered, the man explained with a
bow, to be sent up by Monsieur Wakefield. Despite
herself, Tina was touched. For the first time ever, she
had received a thoughtful gesture from Brant.

On the tray beside the teapot was a slender silver
vase with a single dark-red rose. She lifted the flower
to her nostrils to inhale its heavenly fragrance. Then
she noticed a slip of pasteboard beneath the vase.
Scrawled across it in Brant's large hand, she read, *Tea is
the best restorer of energy! A bientôt!*

So, he could never resist the slightest chance for a
gibe! Tina ignored the tea he'd sent up and lay on the
silk-covered bed under its canopy of filmy drapery. She
felt feather-soft support beneath her weary body,
cradling her restfully. Almost she might have been
drugged from the way her fogged brain craved sleep.
Her last scarcely conscious thought was that she must

have been insane ever to consent to marrying Brant Wakefield.

She woke to the sound of splashing water from the adjoining bathroom. So Brant was back, and taking a shower. Without rising, she bent her arm to see her wristwatch. Almost eight o'clock! Time to get dressed for dinner, though she had no appetite at all.

The shower was turned off and a few moments later Brant appeared in the bathroom doorway. He was wearing a short towelling wrap that scarcely reached to mid-thigh. His dark hair now was curly and even darker from the water, which still clung in glistening droplets to his face and legs. He looked, her treacherous mind registered, piratically handsome.

"Awake?" he greeted her. "You must have gone out like a light. It's the heat, I suppose." Rubbing his hair with a towel, he came nearer and noticed the un-touched teatray. One eyebrow quirked at her in enquiry. Tina stared back at him defiantly, and he shrugged. Already, she realised, there was a great deal they could say to one another without using words.

"What you need is a nice brisk shower," Brant remarked. "I can strongly recommend it for that jaded feeling." Dark eyes glinted wickedly. "It's almost as good as an early morning dip in the lake . . . and less public!"

Tina felt horribly vulnerable lying there on that silk-soft bed. But it was an error of judgment to rise at that moment, because she stepped right into his encircling arms. His hands slid over her back, tracing the ridged curve of her spine, and Tina shivered involuntarily at this new and unexpected note of tenderness. Even though she felt his body quicken against hers, his lips on her hair were very gentle, his kiss a lover's kiss.

This was madness! Was she to be disarmed by a rising

tide of longing at his first casual attempt to break through her defences? Somehow she steeled her resolve, and thrust herself back from him.

"I'll go and have that shower," she murmured briskly.

Brant laughed, but let her go. "Want me to come and soap you?"

"No!" The protest in that one short word was shrill, and he laughed again, softly. "Such maidenly modesty! And quite misplaced, I'm certain—though the nearest I've come to seeing you unadorned was on the night you played Juliet to my Romeo." That hateful note of amusement was deep in his throat as he went on, "In that respect, my darling, you still have the advantage of me! However, it's a state of affairs that I don't propose to allow to continue for much longer, so I'll contain my impatience!"

Tina almost ran in her desperation to escape from him. While she was showering she heard him enter the bathroom, but it was only to toss in the wrap and towel he'd used. Through a tiny slit in the shower door, she watched him walk naked to the bedroom, the muscles of his broad back rippling with every movement.

They dined, not in the hotel restaurant but in a crowded and clearly popular restaurant in the Latin quarter, to which they went by taxi.

"You seem to know your way around Paris," Tina remarked wonderingly, as the headwaiter threaded a path for them to a well placed table near the dance floor.

"A knowledge of Paris is essential equipment for every romantically-bent male," Brant responded with a laugh.

His knowledge of the language, too, put Tina's stumbling efforts to shame. He chose the meal for both of them . . . unhurriedly but decisively, not once questioning whether she might prefer something different. Tina was grateful for the buzz of conversation and the throbbing music from the five-piece combo, which made an atmosphere inimical to the sort of intimate, tête-a-tête dinner she had been so dreading. Brant asked her to dance, taking her acceptance for granted as he swept her onto the small, circular floor. It was crowded, and he held her very close. Afraid of the way her body wanted to melt itself against his—almost as if it had been created for that purpose—she did a brisk run-through in her mind of every unkind action or remark of his since that very first day they had met. Brant must have noticed that she danced stiffly, responding in a mechanical way to his lithely gliding movements, but he made no comment.

They had just returned to their table when a voice behind Tina's chair cried, "Hallo there, what a surprise seeing you two here!"

She twisted her head to see the dinner-jacketed figure of Jocelyn Ashley smiling down at her. "Good evening, Miss Harcourt."

"It's not Miss Harcourt any longer, Jocelyn," Brant explained. "Mrs. Wakefield, if you please—though I'm sure she would be happy for you to call her Tina."

Jocelyn's jaw had dropped. "Mrs. Wakefield! Good Lord, I'm most terribly sorry. . . ." The colour flooding to his face betrayed all too clearly what he had been thinking. "Er . . . my heartiest congratulations to you both."

Brant suggested pleasantly, "Why not join us for a few minutes to drink our health?"

The other man hesitated. "Are you quite sure I wouldn't be *de trop?*"

"Of course not!" That was Tina, and her eager readiness for Jocelyn's company did not pass unnoticed by Brant, whose eyes glinted darkly.

"Well, just for a moment, then," Jocelyn accepted. "Actually, I'm over here with a party of museum people as guests of our French opposite numbers, and we're having a night out." He waved to someone across the room, miming his intention, then sat down. Brant signalled the waiter for a third glass, and when it came and was filled he proposed a toast.

"We'll all drink to one another, shall we? To success in all our endeavours!"

The three glasses clinked across the table, and they sipped the cool white wine. Then Jocelyn remarked with a chuckle, "Well, you're a couple of dark horses, I must say. When I was at Hucclecote Hall you didn't give me the least hint of what was afoot between you."

"We didn't know ourselves, then," Brant explained.

"Oh, yes, of course, at that time you were . . ." Jocelyn quickly backed away from what he had been about to say. It was obvious that he had just remembered Loretta Boyd-French. Mercifully, the flashing strobe lights helped to conceal the colour that rushed to Tina's cheeks, and a crescendo of music called a halt to conversation for the moment.

"Do you think I might be allowed to dance with the beautiful bride?" Jocelyn asked, when it was possible to talk again.

"Go right ahead," Brant acquiesced carelessly.

Yet Tina was conscious that her husband's gaze followed them to the floor. Jocelyn, somewhat to her surprise, was a good dancer, but with him it was a very different matter from dancing with Brant. They remained two individual people, moving together in unison yet each in their own separate world. Jocelyn murmured something to her, and Tina took the chance to glance up at his face with a bright smile . . . a smile intended for the benefit of watching eyes. Then she realised to her confusion that her partner had been praising Brant to the skies.

"He's a really terrific guy!" Jocelyn averred admiringly. "But then you know all about that, Tina, or you wouldn't have married him."

Caught off-guard for the moment, she said something that discretion would have best left unsaid. "I get the idea that a lot of people think I married Brant for his money."

Jocelyn looked startled at such frank speaking, then gave an awkward laugh. "That's ridiculous!" he protested. "A girl with your looks and charm and intelligence could take her pick from the most eligible bachelors going. No, you married Brant Wakefield for one reason and one reason only . . . you're head over heels in love with the chap. That fact is glaringly obvious, Tina. The whole time you've been dancing with me your attention has been on him, right across the room. As for Brant . . . his eyes devour you. And no man could blame him for that."

Tina shivered, and irresistibly her gaze was dragged back to her husband again.

"See what I mean?" Jocelyn chuckled, with an envious little sigh.

Later, as they were returning to their hotel, Brant suggested leaving the taxi and walking the rest of the way. Tina readily agreed, because it would postpone the moment when she faced him alone in their bedroom. This prospect filled her now with ever-mounting dread.

They conversed very little as they strolled along the Seine's left bank, perhaps seeming to observers as much lost in their own private heaven as any other of the numerous couples who sauntered there. They crossed the river by a little iron footbridge, pausing to admire the floodlit buildings on the Île de la Cité, then walked on through the beautiful, peaceful Tuileries gardens until they emerged into the busily whirling traffic of the Place de la Concorde.

A dignified hush cloaked their hotel. Crossing the vast foyer, Brant said suddenly, "I'll have a last drink, I think. Will you go on up?"

At least, Tina thought thankfully, as she ascended alone in the silent lift, she would have a chance to get undressed in peace, and time to compose herself a little. But the thudding of her heartbeat diminished not one whit as the minutes passed. Rather, it seemed to grow in intensity until its throbbing drowned out all other sound. Lying in the great soft bed at last, the silken coverlet drawn up to her chin, the room seemed to be tilting and swaying around her. She wished now that Brant would hurry up and come to her. Surely this sickening dread was worse than the reality could possibly be?

Time dragged on with interminable slowness. Was this another trick of his, another taunt? And then he was there, entering from the sitting room and shutting the door quietly behind him. Tina lay with her eyes closed, listening to him as he moved about the room undressing, running the taps in the bathroom. At long last she felt the bedsprings dip as her husband drew back the covers and slid in beside her, near but not touching.

"It takes a lot of believing, Tina," he remarked in a conversational tone, "that you should be asleep tonight of all nights!"

Abandoning pretence, she said bitterly, "You could hardly blame me if I had dropped off to sleep. You were a long time."

"And you were impatient? Never mind, darling, I'm here now."

She moved, to turn away from him. But his hand closed on her arm, not steel-like this time, but still with the firmness of utter determination. With a single movement of his other hand he threw aside the bedcovers.

"What's this I see?" he drawled. "Such a demure nightdress for a bride on her honeymoon! I must confess you disappoint me, Tina. I was anticipating something far more seductive than this up-to-the-neck and down-to-the-ankles creation. Something see-through and skimpy that conceals just enough to inflame a husband's imagination but not a square inch more. . . ."

"Stop it!" she cried.

"Than remove the offending garment."

"I won't!" she choked.

"You prefer me to do it for you?"

Tina thrashed her body wildly to escape him, but in vain. Her husband moved above her, his naked skin gleaming bronzelike in the glow of the softly-shaded bedside lamp. Skillful fingers found the fastenings of her nightdress and drew it smoothly away as though her struggles were no more than playful wrigglings of pleasure. Then Brant became very still. His face above hers, darkly-shadowed to match the colour of his teak-brown hair, held no mockery now. His eyes were glowing in reverent admiration.

"You are exquisite!" he breathed huskily. "Such flawless perfection!"

He no longer held her prisoner. But Tina was powerless to move a muscle as, feather-lightly, Brant kissed her closed eyelids, her cheeks, the corner of her mouth, his lips moving down to the soft hollows at the base of her throat while his hand gently fondled the silk-smooth skin of her shoulder. Then his lips travelled downward, leaving a burning trail of little kisses till his face was buried deep in the warm, secret valley between her breasts. A low moan of pleasure was torn from her. Involuntarily, her own hands reached out to clasp his neck, her fingers curling into his crisp dark hair while her whole body strove to mould itself ever more closely to his.

"Tina, my beautiful Tina," he murmured chokingly, repeating her name again and again, his hand by now closed possessively over her breast's soft roundness. When he began to make tiny caressing strokes with his thumb, Tina felt her nipples suddenly tighten to hard, sharp points as a flame of hot desire licked through her. . . .

She snapped back to contemptuous awareness, and the contempt was directed at herself. Just so easily could Brant sweep away all that fierce resolve! But she had snatched herself back just in time, before he proved irrevocably that he could arouse her to such heady peaks of passion. As his weight descended upon her in urgent, demanding maleness, she steeled her body to become a slab of cold ice. She would resist nothing, but she would yield nothing! What her husband wanted he must take, in the full knowledge that she despised him.

"Why do you fight me, Tina?" he demanded thickly.

"I am not fighting you," she said. "And I don't intend to—ever."

"Why do you fight yourself, then?" he amended. "For just a few moments there was truth and honesty between us. And then. . . ."

"No, not truth and honesty," she denied. "There can never be that, not in a marriage such as ours."

She heard his sharp intake of breath, and powerful fingers dug cruelly into the soft flesh of her shoulders.

"You are my wife!" he ground out.

"That doesn't mean that you own me," she countered.

He seemed to abandon the last remnants of self-control. His weight was crushing her, his strength overwhelming her mercilessly.

"I do own you," he hissed. "If this is the way you insist that it's got to be, Tina, then I bought you, like any other commodity. I bought you body and soul."

"No!" she cried wildly. "You may have bought my body, Brant, and I won't deny it to you . . . not now, not ever, so take what you want! But my soul is my own, and it will never be yours—not for as long as I live."

Tina flinched away from the look of baffled fury in his eyes, but she had to go on flinging out her pent-up bitterness.

"Is that what eats you up, Brant . . . the knowledge that all you've ever had from any of your mistresses was bought with money? You contemptuously reject the idea of love between a man and a woman, yet you have the gall to expect submissive adoration from me now. Well, you can go on expecting! You'll only ever get back as much as you're prepared to give!"

His breath was rasping, and she could feel the pulses throbbing through his body. Then, suddenly, his crushing weight was gone from her. He stood beside the bed, dragging on his robe, an immensely tall and ominous figure from where she lay.

"Damn you, Tina!" he gritted. "Damn you to hell! You say that I own your body, but I prefer not to take delivery on the terms you offer. I won't pretend I don't want you—right now, perhaps, more than ever. But if I have to suffer, then so, by God, will you! You can't deceive me that your body isn't every bit as much on fire as mine is, but I'm not going to humiliate myself just to satisfy your twisted puritanism. You'll have to plead with me, my dear sweet wife, before I ever so much as touch you again."

He stood looking down at her for a moment longer, his lips curled in scorn. Then he turned on his heel and strode to the door of the sitting room. It slammed behind him, and there was silence.

For minutes more Tina lay utterly still. Then, very slowly, she reached down and dragged the covers up to hide her nakedness. Her weeping continued long into the night.

Chapter Eleven

Those honeymoon days they spent in Paris had all the unreality of a dream, a dream that was not entirely a nightmare. Brant made no further reference to the scene in their bedroom on that first night. He remained cool and distant—though invariably courteous. It was an interval of unnatural calm—the calm eye of the storm, perhaps? Would they, one or the other of them, make an unwary move that would instantly plunge them back into the hurricane? There were times when Tina almost wished it would happen . . . anything rather than this curious, cautiously-circling relationship of two strangers.

And yet, as they roamed Paris on sightseeing trips, there were moments when their enmity seemed to melt away and they would find themselves talking without reserve about something that had caught their interest. Once, leaning idly on the parapet of a bridge over the Seine, they even laughed at the antics of a group of small boys in swimtrunks who were fooling about and shoving one another into the water with shrieks of delight.

"One almost envies them," Brant commented. Did he mean that he envied them the chance to wear next-to-nothing and splash about in the cool water on this scorcher of a day? Or was he saying that he envied them the innocent happiness of childhood, when the worst problems were a cut knee or a treat denied?

But this moment of nearness, their shared smile, had to be paid for. When they strolled on again, with the twin towers of the lovely Notre Dame Cathedral rising above them, they seemed somehow further apart than ever. They stopped at a little sidewalk café that was shielded from the blazing sun by a gaily-striped awning, and they might have been married for long dreary years for all the attention they paid each other. After ordering their coffee, Brant sat absorbed in a copy of *Le Monde* while Tina was left to tap her fingers restlessly on the little round table and think her own unhappy thoughts.

They visited the Louvre, and she gazed long and searchingly at the Mona Lisa, trying to pierce the elusive sadness which lay behind the wistfully enigmatic smile of Leonardo da Vinci's masterpiece. She felt herself curiously at one with the woman in the portrait.

Beside her, Brant murmured, "It's a fantastic work of art, isn't it?"

Tina nodded, unable to put her own feelings into words. They gathered in her throat as a painful lump.

She and Brant did the rounds of the other sights. They went to cosmopolitan Montmartre and the Sacre Coeur, that lovely white-domed basilica perched proudly upon its small hill, to the Arc de Triomphe and the tomb of the unknown soldier, with its flickering flame of eternal remembrance. They ascended to the topmost stage of the Eiffel Tower for a breathtaking panorama of Paris and its environs, and went to Les Invalides to see the Emperor Napoleon's final resting place. A longer trip by hired car took them out to Versailles, the magnificent royal palace that was the conception of Paris-hating Louis the Fourteenth, and further embellished by his son, the fifteenth Louis, who was aided in the task by his beautiful and beloved mistress, Madame de Pompadour. Tina had never before seen such rich splendour as in those spacious apartments, nor such elaborate formality as in the palace gardens, laid out with huge stone sculptures, ornamental fountains and dashing cascades of water.

On the final evening of this thankfully-brief honeymoon, they dined quietly in the hotel's ornate restaurant. Because they occupied the bridal suite the management had put a vase of red roses on their table. And on this last evening a bottle of vintage champagne was provided with respectful compliments.

Twirling a glass in his fingers, watching the bubbles rising in a steady stream, Brant remarked, "There'll be a big pile-up of work waiting for me when we get back tomorrow."

"I'll be able to help you," Tina said quickly.

The expression in his dark eyes was faintly puzzled. "You intend to keep on with the book, don't you?"

"Oh yes," she confirmed. "But there'll be lots of other things I can handle for you, I'm sure."

He was silent, frowning. Then he said, "You don't have to help with the estate, you know, Tina. I don't necessarily expect. . . ."

"As long as I'm your wife," she broke in, "I shall take my duties seriously."

He continued to look at her, his face almost expressionless. Tina again had that strange feeling she had experienced so often this past week . . . that they could read each other's mind without the need for words. That words, in fact, only served to obscure the real issues that lay between them.

Eventually, he breathed very softly, "You mean you'll do your duty in every sense but one?"

"No!" she flashed. "In *every* sense! I have made that clear."

"Ah yes," he murmured, with bitter irony, "you will suffer me to make love to you, right?"

"Make *love?*" she echoed scornfully. "I wonder you dare use that word, in whatever context."

His dark eyes glittered dangerously, reflecting the myriad crystal drops of the huge chandelier above their heads. But his voice was lazy as he drawled, "Let's not quibble over one word, Tina, when we have so much else to fight about."

"I don't want to fight you, Brant," she protested.

"No, that's right! Passive acquiescence is the order of the day. I am to be permitted a husband's conjugal rights—that, and not one iota more." His eyes narrowed, surveying her secretively from under long, thick lashes. "In point of fact, my dearest Tina, until I have availed myself of your generous offer, I cannot truly call myself your husband. Is that not so?"

She didn't know how to answer him, and she stared down at her plate nervously. Brant did not refer to the subject again over the meal, talking instead of the afternoon's outing to the royal palace at Fontainbleau in its romantically wild setting of an ancient forest, and afterwards to the pretty Château de Malmaison where Napoleon had spent happy years with his adored Josephine.

But when the meal was over, Brant rose to his feet and said casually, "Shall we go?"

Tina rose too, expecting him to suggest going through to one of the several lounges. Instead, he headed for the lift. Wondering a little, she found herself being wafted upstairs with him.

"A bath, and then bed, I think," he recommended.

It was scarcely ten o'clock, but she acquiesced

without demur. She had grown accustomed now to
sleeping alone in the great wide bed which she had
expected to share with her husband, that voluptuously
luxurious stage for the intimacies of marriage. No
reference was ever made between them to the fact that
Brant left her each night to sleep on the couch in the
adjoining sitting room of their suite. Tina would bid
him goodnight with a curious mixture of emotions,
primarily relief but also a certain resentment, even a
faint wistfulness.

Tonight, Brant said, "About the bath . . . will you go
first, or shall I?"

"You," she opted quickly. That meant he would be
out of the way by the time she had hers, and she could
enjoy a relaxing soak in peace.

She spent the quarter of an hour while Brant was in
the bath packing some of her things in readiness for
their departure the next day. When he came back to the
bedroom in his robe and started hanging his clothes in
the wardrobe, she herself made for the bathroom,
saying goodnight as she went. He grunted in reply.

A few minutes later, when she was lying back
luxuriously in the warm, scented water, she was jolted
with alarm when the door suddenly opened and Brant
strolled in. He barely glanced at her, explaining
casually, "Thought I'd better have another shave."

There was nothing Tina could do. Thankful, at least,
that the bath water was concealingly deep and bubbly
she lay there wretchedly and listened to the quiet buzz
of his shaver. She knew why he was doing this, of
course. To humiliate her! To indicate that he had access
to her nakedness whenever and wherever he chose.
That she had no privacy from him.

The langorous pleasure of her bath was utterly
destroyed, As soon as Brant had departed she quickly

soaped herself, rinsed, and stepped out, enveloping herself immediately in a huge bath towel in case he took it into his head to burst in upon her a second time. To have slipped the catch on the door, she knew with unhappy certainty, would only have given him cause for further sarcasm.

Everything was silent in this hushed and discreet hotel, even the noise of traffic on the nearby Place de la Concorde was reduced to a mere whisper by the double-paned windows and heavy damask drapes. The air conditioning kept the temperature pleasantly cool after the fierce heat of the day.

Slipping into her nightdress, Tina opened the door and walked through into the bedroom. Then she stopped in dismay. Lying upon the bed, fingers linked behind his head, was Brant. He wore only his short silk robe, his long bare legs stretched out and crossed at the ankles.

"So!" he greeted her. "Another passion-killer of a nightdress! Where *do* you find them, Tina?"

"What . . . what are you doing here?" she faltered confusedly.

His eyes widened in mocking reproach. "What a question for a wife to ask her husband. What is he doing on the marriage bed?"

"But I . . . I thought. . . ."

"Whatever you thought," he drawled, "it seems you thought wrong! There's the little matter I mentioned over dinner to be attended to . . . the setting of the seal upon our marriage. I wouldn't want you ever to get it into your pretty head that you could obtain an annulment."

Anger surged over her, forcing all other feelings away.

"You're despicable!" she spat at him. "You marry me quite blatantly for the sole purpose of securing your inheritance, and now you want to make sure that nothing can possibly go wrong, by . . . by . . ."

"By what?" he taunted.

"By *this!*" she flared. "Well, you needn't think I'm going to meekly succumb."

"You assured me that 'succumb' is precisely what you would do," he reminded her. "Not an hour ago you stated very forcefully that you were prepared to do your duty as a wife in *every* sense."

"But I didn't mean . . . not like this. Not coldly calculating, merely to establish a legal point."

Brant sprang up from the bed and came to her, his handsome face twisted with rage. "Get this into your head—sweetheart! I'll take whatever I want from you how I want it and when I want it. Clear? And that's going to be *now!*"

She stepped back quickly, cowering away from him. But Brant was upon her, his hands brutally rough as he tore the offending nightdress from her body, his own robe following it to the floor. She gave a low moan of fear as he swept her up and carried her to the bed, flinging her down and himself on top of her. She fought back desperately, but she was powerless to resist the unbridled strength he used against her. Without pity and without mercy he took possession of her, invading her with a barbarous force that made her cry out in pain. And then, incredibly, through her shrinking fear came the traitorous reaction from her body that she had so dreaded, had so firmly resolved to keep in subjugation. Her hands no longer fought him, but clung urgently and tried to draw him even closer. Her mind was a swirling mist of mounting desire which obliterated all thought, all resolution, every last trace of shame.

When, finally, Brant flung himself aside, she felt bereft. He lay heavily beside her, not touching her, his breathing deep and fast. Shame came creeping back to her then, filtering through the obscuring haze in her mind. It shocked her profoundly that she had found joy, even ecstasy, in that hateful, obscene act of consummation which was such a ghastly parody of the act of love.

She felt Brant move, and became dimly aware of dark eyes glittering at her in the soft lamplight.

"Are you all right, Tina?"

She didn't reply. There seemed nothing to say. After a moment he went on roughly, "You asked for it, you can't pretend you didn't." Another pause, then, "What the hell! *You* wanted *me,* too, just as you always have done. Well, make no mistake about this, my dear Tina . . . if you want any more from me you're going to have to come crawling for it."

"Never!" The single word came as a croak from far away.

"Never is a long time to deny yourself, wife!" he said, cruel mockery back in his voice. "You may look at me with loathing in those beautiful blue eyes of yours, but you're fighting a losing battle against your own instincts. You know I'm right."

With eyelids closed, Tina felt the mattress tilt as he rose from the bed. She heard him walk across the room, flinched as the dividing door slammed violently behind him. She opened her eyes and lay staring up at the ornate ceiling, where ominous shadows seemed to be gathering. If Brant had shown me just a trace of tenderness, she thought wistfully, if he had murmured one single word of endearment, perhaps I wouldn't need to despise myself so much. But even though he had violated her with uncaring savagery, intent only on ensuring that she was incontestably his wife, she had nevertheless responded. Brant had awakened in her once again—as he had gloated in demonstrating that he always could—the primitive sexuality with which she was burdened.

She began to shiver uncontrollably. Then slowly, as if performing a difficult feat, she lifted the covers and slid into bed, curling her arms and slender body into a tightknit ball as though in feeble defence against a cruelly hostile world.

Chapter Twelve

It was possible, Tina discovered to her surprise as day followed day, to make some sort of life for herself from out of the disastrous wreckage of her marriage.

There was much to be endured, of course, in addition to her miserable relationship with Brant. For instance, the incredulous look in Mrs. Moncrieff's eyes when, after joyfully greeting the homecoming honeymooners, it had been borne upon her that Tina alone would be occupying the charming double bedroom she had prepared for them both, Brant intending to spend his nights in his former bachelor bedroom.

Naturally this regrettable, but intriguing, item of news wasn't long in spreading round the estate—and the village too, no doubt. Wherever she went, Tina felt watched by speculative eyes. It was something which made every outing an ordeal to be faced. But on the positive side, she found that returning to her research work in the library came as a pleasurable relief from all this. She spent every hour she could spare in the restful room, absorbed in the multitude of old records and documents concerning the ancient family to which she now belonged.

She had made it clear to Brant, however, that she was ready to drop her own work at any time, in order to help him with the more immediate task of getting the estate into shape and preparing for the opening of the house and gardens to the public next spring. To Tina's surprise (and his as well, she suspected) during these times of working together they achieved a harmonious relationship which enabled them to get a considerable amount done. Once, when she had run an elusive craftsmen to earth, a straw thatcher, and pinned him down to an early date for re-roofing the wheelwright's shop, Brant had said admiringly, "I'd pretty well given up hope of getting that job done, Tina. Heaven knows how I'd ever manage without you!" She felt a warm glow stealing over her, and turned her face away so that he wouldn't see her flushed cheeks.

On another occasion, too, she was warmed by her husband's approval when the news arrived that she had indeed been awarded the first class degree which Charles had always predicted for her. Tina herself had been somewhat less confident, and she felt relief and pleasure at being able to win Brant's unfeigned congratulations.

For most of the time, it had to be admitted, he behaved towards her with perfect courtesy. On the day the stallion which Brant had purchased before their marriage was delivered to Hucclecote Hall in a horse-box, he asked Tina to come out with him for her first riding lesson. And after that, they managed to fit in at least half an hour in the saddle most days. The mare she had chosen for herself, a lovely little chestnut Connemara pony just over thirteen hands high named Kirsty, looked so incredibly delicate stepping along beside Brant's giant mount, Heracles. And yet, when she and Brant happened to pause so he could correct her position in the saddle or her grip on the reins, Tina noticed how the great stallion and the little mare would nuzzle each other affectionately.

One afternoon, when Brant had gone to London for

the day to see his accountant, she went riding alone. Already she felt quite safe at a gentle trot, but today, in deference to the heat, she let Kirsty wend her way at a walk through the little silver birch wood that hugged the end of the lake. Yet even here, by the water, there was no breeze to be found, and Tina felt drugged by the breathless stillness. It was entirely due to her own inattention, she acknowledged to herself at once, that she was wrenched from the saddle by a low, springy branch. For a few moments she lay where she had fallen, all the breath knocked from her body. Then, gingerly, she tried to get to her feet but a piercing pain in her left ankle soon put a stop to that. Tina sat down again ruefully, hoping that it was no more than a sprain and wondering how long it would be before someone happened along. The little mare, after wandering around her somewhat bewilderedly, soon settled to cropping the nearby grass.

Fortunately, as long as Tina kept her leg quite still, the pain wasn't too severe. Her drowsiness returned, augmented perhaps by the shock of the fall. Her eyelids were drooping when she heard footsteps approaching, and she glanced up to see Jeff Lintott.

At first he didn't realise that anything was wrong. "Hallo, Tina," he greeted her awkwardly, because like everyone else he was well aware that things were badly wrong between her and Brant. "Having a little snooze on this warm afternoon?"

"No," she explained, giving him an apologetic smile. "I fell off Kirsty and I've twisted my ankle."

"Oh, good Lord!" Jeff dropped on one knee. "Which ankle is it?" She told him, and he probed it with surprisingly gentle fingers, easing up the leg of her jeans a few inches. Careful though he was, Tina couldn't help an occasional wince. In the end he pronounced, "This needs attention. I'd better get you to my farmhouse; it's much nearer than the Hall itself."

"But I can't put my weight on it," she protested.

Jeff smiled with all the complacence of a huskily-built six footer. "Don't worry, I'm going to carry you."

He lifted her with the greatest ease, clucked at Kirsty to follow, and strode with her through the trees. They reached the farmhouse in hardly more than three minutes, and Jeff laid her down carefully on the old stuffed sofa in the farm kitchen, a sofa on which, he told her, he liked to put his feet up and watch TV after a hard day's work around the farm.

"Now then," he said, "I think a nip of brandy is indicated."

Tina shook her head. "No, I'd rather not, Jeff."

"Well then, a restorative cup of tea. I'll just fill the kettle."

Having done that, he went off to fetch his first-aid kit. Returning, he had a thoughtful air.

"You know, Tina, I wonder if I shouldn't phone for Dr. Rowley to come and look at that ankle."

"Oh, but it's only a slight sprain, surely? And she must be terribly busy, having only recently taken over the practice."

"I'm sure she wouldn't mind coming, though," Jeff assured her. "Nothing seems too much trouble for our Dr. Rowley. She's extremely conscientious."

Glancing quickly at his earnest face, Tina wondered if perhaps Jeff had fallen for the new village doctor. It really wouldn't be surprising. Gillian Rowley, somewhere in her early thirties, was a charming woman, as well as having impressed the locality with her dedication and medical skill. But Tina would feel a fraud to summon the overworked doctor without good cause, so she vetoed Jeff's suggestion.

"If you could just put a cold compress on my ankle for now, I'm sure that it'll be okay by tomorrow," she insisted, adding, "I'm afraid I'll have to ask you to drive me home, though."

The cold bandage soaked in witchhazel was remarkably soothing, and the cup of tea worked wonders. Tina actually enjoyed a slice of Mrs. Moncreiff's excellent walnut cake, though lately she had been eating rather from a sense of necessity than for pleasure. The whole atmosphere here, in fact, plus Jeff's pleasant, friendly face, engendered in her a feeling of calmness and relaxation. She realised just how tensed-up she had become since her marriage. Presently, she even found herself talking about her unhappy relationship with Brant.

It was Jeff who brought the subject up. Stirring his second cup of tea with more vigour than necessary, he suddenly burst out, "Look, I know it's none of my business, Tina, but . . ." There was a pause and he started over again. "Hell, it *is* my business in a way . . . I mean, when things go wrong between two people you care about. . . ."

Tina waited, her heart beating very fast, and he finally managed to finish, "Well, it's painfully obvious that things aren't too good between you and Brant. Are they?"

"They're not ideal," she conceded warily.

"Anything I can do to help?" Jeff asked, his expression serious and concerned. "Anything at all? You'd only have to say the word, Tina."

She reached out and touched his large brown hand in a gesture of appreciation. "I know, Jeff! But honestly, I don't think. . . ."

Outside the window she could see Kirsty contentedly grazing the short grass where Jeff had loosely tethered her to the gatepost. Beyond, the rolling meadowland was golden with ripening wheat. Further away still, the softly-ridged line of the Downs was a dark bluish-green against the sun-filled sky.

Jeff's next words echoed her own wistful thoughts. "Everything could be so perfect," he mused unhappily. "When I heard you and Brant were getting married, I was really delighted. That Loretta Boyd-French—she'd have been a dead loss, but I reckoned that you and Brant would make a great team. And so you do, in the way of getting things moving here, but. . . ."

"Perhaps we'll just have to settle for that much," Tina murmured sorrowfully. "Considering the reason that Brant married me."

"The reason?" Jeff echoed, looking puzzled. Then, light dawning, he queried, "Oh, you mean because of the terms of the Wakefield inheritance?"

She nodded, moistening her dry lips, and he went on fervently, "Anyone with the least inkling of what makes people like you and Brant tick would know that it's a crazy idea. I wonder sometimes if he would ever have gone through with marrying Loretta when it came to the crunch . . . not once he'd met you." Jeff paused, looking at her intently. "If you imagine that Brant asked you to marry him for any reason except that he loves you . . . forget it! He's a really great guy, Tina . . . the most genuine, straightforward man I know."

Everyone was so full of adulation for Brant, she thought forlornly. Jeff, Mrs. Moncrieff, the two village women who came to do the routine cleaning of the great house, plus all the workers on the estate and his wealthy neighbours. Even Jocelyn Ashley, who was an outsider. But not one of them had seen the converse side of her husband's nature . . . the cruel, sadistic side of him that found pleasure in tormenting her.

She indicated to Jeff that she would prefer to let the subject drop, and they talked of other things. Jeff

mentioned the coming fete in aid of the Cottage
Hosptial and related a hilarious story of how, last
summer, the specially-erected wooden platform had
slowly subsided under the weight of the village band,
stout fellows all, and how they'd gamely kept on
oom-pah-pahing to the bitter end. Quite taken out of
herself for the moment, Tina was curled up with
laughter when a shadow darkened the window of the
farmhouse kitchen. A moment later Brant stooped
through the low doorway. In a single swift glance he
assessed the situation . . . Tina reclining on the sofa,
Jeff with his chair drawn up close.

"I saw Kirsty tethered outside," he informed them,
his expression chillingly cold. "So I presumed that I
would find you in here."

Jeff had risen quickly to his feet, while Tina stammered, "You're back early, Brant!"

"Aren't I?" he agreed sarcastically.

"I took a tumble off Kirsty," she hastened to explain.
"Jeff found me in the woods and brought me here
because it was nearest."

"I see that your ankle is bandaged," Brant commented.

"It's nothing, really," she said dismissively. "Just a
slight sprain. The swelling has gone down a lot already."

There was an awkward silence, which Jeff filled by
asking Brant if he'd like a cup of tea. "I can easily make
a fresh pot."

The answer was a curt brush-off. "Thanks, but I'd
prefer not to stay. In any case, you must have plenty to
get on with." Brant glanced down at Tina. "I'd better
carry you, it's not worth fetching a car."

"I think I can walk," she said quickly. The thought of
being carried all the way back to the house in Brant's

arms filled her with panic. Since that last night of their honeymoon, the only times they had so much as touched were an accidental brushing of fingers while they were working, or when he was helping her mount Kirsty. But held cradled closely against his body, she was afraid that her perilously-balanced emotional stability would be upset. That, once again, without really trying to, Brant would demonstrate the shattering effect he had on her.

"You seem to have made a remarkably speedy recovery," Brant observed sardonically. "To what must it be attributed, do you think . . . the healing power of Jeff's hands?"

The estate bailiff gave his boss an embarrassed glance. "These sprains sometimes blow up very quickly, and go down just as fast," he said uneasily.

Tina was afraid that her husband might say something really accusing to Jeff, so she hastily stood up and took an experimental step or two, thankful that she hadn't let Jeff remove her shoe. With her full weight on the ankle, it immediately started to throb again, but she wouldn't have admitted that for worlds.

"Thanks for the tea, Jeff," she said, forcing a bright smile. "And for the bandage, it's really worked wonders."

"Hasn't it just!" Brant observed, watching her walk across the room to the door. With a barked, "See you, Jeff!" he followed her out.

By the time they had reached the big house, Tina's one thought was to find somewhere to sit down. But once inside the Great Hall, Brant stayed her by catching at her arm.

"Just what was that all about?" he enquired, his voice dangerously smooth.

"I've already told you," she replied wearily.

His lips were sneering. "I noticed that you walked quite normally—except when you remembered to limp a few steps for my benefit."

Tina stared at him in dismay. The truth was completely the reverse. She had forced herself to walk normally, except when her guard was momentarily down and the pain had caught her unawares.

"You lost no time in resuming your intimate little tea-parties in Jeff's house," he accused her with cold fury. "The first day I'm away for any length of time, and there you are!"

"Oh, this is ridiculous," Tina began, and turned to walk away from him. But her ankle gave a sharp warning stab, which brought her to a halt with a little gasp of pain. "Are you suggesting that my hurt ankle is a piece of fiction?" she demanded.

His slaty eyes were narrowed as he tried to bore into her mind.

"Debatable, I'd say," he commented at length.

Tina drew herself up and said stiffly, "Can you really believe that Jeff and I would invent a story like that, to cover up . . .?"

Brant cut across her, "Not Jeff, not for one moment. He's as straight as a die. But he's susceptible, like most men . . . more than most, poor devil, having lost the wife he adored. So when he comes across a beautiful damsel in distress, who has apparently fallen from her mount, he naturally hastens to the rescue."

"Apparently!" Tina echoed indignantly. "I *did* fall! And I must have bruises all over me to prove it."

"Is that an invitation?" Brant drawled, his eyes lazily running down the length of her figure and up again. "But then, Tina, I'm not susceptible to your feminine wiles, so it won't work with me."

The insistent throbbing in her ankle was getting

worse every moment. But to walk away now would be to concede.

"You can't honestly believe that Jeff is the slightest bit interested in me as a woman," she said beseechingly.

"Are you suggesting that he isn't?" Brant tossed back.

Under the challenge of his gaze, she glanced away uneasily. Dare she make a flat denial? In those earlier meetings between herself and Jeff, the little tea parties at his farmhouse and the visit to the village pub, she had more than once seen him glance at her in a way that suggested intense admiration. And although, since the announcement of her engagement to Brant, he had behaved with the utmost propriety, she recalled how gently his work-roughened hands had probed her ankle for a fracture, how concerned the look in his serious grey eyes had been.

Brant didn't miss her hesitation. He said roughly, "You'd better take this as a warning, Tina . . . I'm not having you giving Jeff a big come-on. He's just about the finest bailiff I could have here, and he's totally loyal. But every man has his limits, and poor Jeff might find himself succumbing, despite himself. You may imagine that leading him on is a clever way of getting back at me, but just get this into your head. If the worst *did* happen, then Jeff would have to go—because I'm damned if I'll be cuckolded on my own doorstep!" His grim expression eased into a smile that was equally as grim. "And don't tell me you've never heard that word before, Tina, not with all your researches into the history of families like mine."

Tina's heart plunged. She knew that Brant was perfectly serious in what he threatened. If he chose to form the wrong impression about her friendship with his bailiff, Jeff Lintott might find himself out of a job. Then a solution seemed to drop down to her from heaven, and she seized upon it eagerly.

"Jeff wouldn't look twice at me," she protested, "even if I wasn't married to you. There's only one woman he's got eyes for right now."

"Who's that?" Brant demanded, his voice heavy with suspicion.

"Why, the new village doctor—Gillian Rowley."

"The *doctor?*" He sounded incredulous.

"Yes, and why not? She's very attractive, and ideal for Jeff agewise . . . about thirty-five, I should think. You remember, Brant, we met her at church a couple of Sundays ago. As a matter of fact," she improvised rapidly, "I was going to suggest that we invite them both to dinner next Tuesday when the Fabers are coming . . . just to help things along. You wouldn't object?"

Her husband looked thoughtful, then shrugged his broad shoulders. "No, why should I?" He hesitated a moment, then enquired, "Do you want me to give you a hand up the stairs?"

Oh, the bliss of being wafted straight up to her bedroom without the need to put her foot wincingly to the floor again! But the fear of Brant was still in her, the fear of his closeness with that warm male scent of him tangling enticingly into her senses. . . .

Tina's anger at herself made her refusal sharper than she intended. "No thank you," she snapped. "I can manage perfectly well on my own."

"Just as you wish!" Brant said indifferently. "I'd hate to impose myself on you—in any way!"

Leaving her, he made for the stairs and took them two at a time, looking immaculate in the light grey suit he'd worn for his London trip. Tina watched him until he was out of sight, then limped wretchedly into the library where, with her left leg propped on a cushioned chair, she could make a pretence of working. It was more than half an hour before the throbbing eased sufficiently for her to face mounting the stairs herself.

Chapter Thirteen

Paul and Harriet Faber, in their mid-thirties and married for more than twelve years—with, back home in Brighton, a boy of ten and a girl of eight to show for it—were still deeply in love. That fact was quite unmistakable. Although they didn't make a big display of it, Tina couldn't avoid noticing how they never seemed to go longer than a minute without finding an opportunity to touch hands or exchange a private smile.

Such a wonderfully happy couple naturally assumed, on the evening they came to dinner at Hucclecote Hall, that the same blissful state of affairs existed between their newly-married host and hostess. Living some distance away, the rumours of a rift hadn't reached them.

Paul and Harriet were by profession theatrical designers. And, as an absorbing hobby, they had become very knowledgeable about the history of costume. It was for this latter expertise that Brant had first got in touch with the couple and a friendship had rapidly developed.

Jeff Lintott and Gillian Rowley, tacked onto the dinner party by Tina as a desperate measure to lull her husband's suspicions, were slightly shy of one another because anybody with half an eye could see that there was matchmaking afoot. But neither of them seemed averse to the idea, to judge by the way their glances kept interlocking. And perhaps, Tina hoped forlornly, those disturbing, dark-lidded glances that Brant kept throwing at her down the length of the dining table, were misconstrued by their guests as the secret look of love.

The subject being discussed over dinner was the forthcoming banquet planned for press and media people. It was to be held in a few weeks' time, to gain publicity for the opening of Hucclecote Hall to the public next spring. It was to be a costume affair, but which particular period had not yet been decided.

"For a house with as long a history as this," Brant remarked, "any century would be equally appropriate."

"Which gives us a nice wide choice," approved Harriet. She was one of those fortunate women whose crisp professionalism did nothing to mar her essential femininity. "Personally, I'd push for the Elizabethan period . . . the women in farthingales and ruffs and the men in doublets and hose."

"What's a farthingale?" asked Jeff.

"It's a bit like a crinoline," Gillian explained. "You know, a very wide skirt held out by a frame. The woman must have had quite a job negotiating doorways in them."

The two exchanged a warm look, and Tina knew that Jeff was pleased it was Gillian who'd answered his question.

Brant was frowning doubtfully. "Wouldn't present-day women prefer the chance to exhibit their charms to better advantage at our banquet?" he queried. "Ruffs sound a bit prim and proper to me."

Harriet gurgled with amusement. "Don't you believe it! Those Elizabethan ladies knew all there was to know about being seductive. A discreet—or maybe not so discreet!—opening at the front of the ruff to expose an expanse of bare bosom worked wonders on the menfolk."

"I can imagine!" Brant laughed. But his dark eyes, fixed on Tina, were not laughing. "I think you've convinced us, Harriet," he went on. "Elizabethan it shall be, then."

"Hold your horses," Paul put in with a rueful grin. "It's all very well for a magnificent, swashbuckling type like you, Brant, to talk blithely of appearing in doublet and hose. But spare a thought for a miserable skin-and-bone specimen of manhood like me."

"Just let anyone else call you that!" his wife threatened, awarding him a loving look across the table. "Never mind, darling, a little bit of padding here and there and we'll make a veritable Sir Walter Raleigh out of you!"

It was agreed that Paul and Harriet should prepare some sketches, and the conversation drifted on to future plans. These costume banquets were to be a regular feature at Hucclecote Hall, when whole haunches of beef and venison and roasted fowl of all kinds would feature on the menu, with mead and sherry sack to be quaffed from pewter tankards, served by girls from the village dressed as merry wenches.

"The public will love it, and you'll be flooded with applications for tickets," Paul affirmed. "The setting couldn't be better than your Great Hall, with smoky tallow candles and straw strewn all over the floor."

His wife giggled. "Darling, you sometimes carry your love of realism a shade too far," she reproved him. "Brant and Tina don't want to risk having their beautiful home burnt to the ground."

The four guests departed soon after eleven, Paul and Harriet having to get back to Brighton to relieve their babysitter. Jeff had walked over from the farmhouse, but Tina, standing unobtrusively at a window of the Great Hall, noticed that he lingered for quite a while by Gillian's car. A romance had started there, undoubtedly, and she knew she was entitled to take much of the credit. She had pointed Jeff in the direction of happiness—something, she thought wistfully, that she was unable to do for herself.

Was she asking too much of life? she wondered, with a despondent sigh. Was she vainly seeking perfection in an imperfect world? Perhaps she'd be wise to accept the terrible flaw in her nature. She and Brant were two of a kind, weren't they, so why not acknowledge this fact? Abandon unattainable dreams of love, and settle instead for what her husband offered in the place of love? That was the point, surely . . . he *was* her lawful husband, so it couldn't be altogether wrong.

Truth and honesty between them, that's what Brant had asked of her. If only truth and honesty meant a coming together in love, as she knew it was for Paul and Harriet, as, in the fullness of time, it was going to be for Jeff and Gillian. But Brant didn't love her, and how could she ever learn to love a man who treated her so cruelly, a man who admitted that their marriage was a mere technical convenience, and an easy way to sexual gratification?

To retract her fervent declaration and go to Brant's arms willingly, to respond to his lovemaking as he'd demanded she should, would only make her despise herself utterly. But already she despised herself beyond redemption for the urgent longings that surged through her whenever she looked at him, whenever she so much as thought about him. How Brant would gloat if she capitulated, but let him gloat! On his terms, at least she would not have to suffer what she was suffering now. If she was a wanton by nature, nothing was going to alter that deplorable fact. She envisioned how it might have been on the first night of their honeymoon, if she had let herself accept Brant's lovemaking on the same terms as it had been made. If, instead of steeling herself against the screaming needs of her body, she had given free rein to the passion he aroused in her. . . .

Tina shivered violently, and hugged her shoulders where her evening gown of white crepe left them bared. She turned from the window and was startled to see, in the shadowed light cast by wall sconces, the tall, leanly powerful figure of the man who had been dominating her thoughts. Brant stood in the archway leading to the staircase hall, his gaze intent.

"You were miles away," he commented.

Yes, she nodded in silent acknowledgement, I was miles away in a luxurious bridal suite of a Paris hotel, thinking sadly of how things might have been. How things still might be, if only . . .

She would have to go crawling to him, Brant had threatened, before he would ever touch her again. She couldn't bring herself to crawl, though, she couldn't! She still had too much pride left for that. But surely, if he truly desired her body as he'd repeatedly claimed, then she only had to convey to him that he wouldn't be spurned in future? Convey in the small, subtle ways that any woman can communicate this to a man?

Her heart hammering with expectation, Tina slowly crossed the marble floor towards him, and smiled.

"It was a good evening, Brant, wasn't it?" she murmured softly.

"Yes, we achieved quite a lot. Paul and Harriet are proving very helpful."

"They're a really nice couple, too," Tina added, with a dreamy sigh.

Brant agreed with her again, but looked at her oddly, trying to assess this subtle change in her mood.

"It must be lovely for them," she enlarged, "sharing

the same interests the way they do. Theirs is truly a marriage of kindred spirits."

She had walked past him, and now began to mount the stairs, a slight twinge in the ankle reminding her of her accident last week. Brant followed, a step or two behind. The old grandfather clock stirred into ponderous life and chimed the half-hour, then lapsed back to its steady ticking.

Upstairs in the apartment it was very quiet. Mrs. Moncrieff, having cooked and served an elaborate dinner for six, had retired thankfully to bed. Tina paused when she reached the drawing room door, and turned back to face her husband.

"Is there anything I can get for you, Brant?" she asked tremulously.

"Such as?" His dark eyes were wary.

"Some coffee?" she suggested. "A last drink?"

"Since when have you been so solicitous about my needs?" he enquired drily.

He was standing very close, scarcely a foot away, as if deliberately provoking her with his magnetic nearness. If only, she thought, he would reach out and sweep her into his arms. All her scruples would be cast aside, all her bitter self-condemnation. She was ready to abandon herself to the dizzy exultation of the senses, as Brant had demanded she should. She would allow her sensuous body to have its way and reach the only kind of fulfilment, it seemed, of which she was capable. He must, surely, be able to hear her thudding heartbeat that grew louder and faster second by second like the summons of a tribal war drum. So why, then, did he torment her so by standing there unmoving, his dark eyes slitted?

She managed huskily, with a shrug of her slender shoulders, "If wives can't be solicitous towards their husbands . . ."

"Don't generalise!" he rebuked her sharply. "We're talking about *us.*"

"I . . . I was just trying to be pleasant," she said weakly.

"Correction, I think," he drawled. "You're trying to be seductive, aren't you, sweetheart? What's the trouble, is your resolution wearing thin at last?"

She winced, as if he'd struck her across the face. "Must you always be so crude?"

"Oh, I was forgetting," he sneered. "You like a nice coating of sugar icing on your sex, don't you?" Reaching out, he grasped her wrist in that achingly familiar grip of steel. "What's this little scene all about, I'd like to know? Does it amuse your twisted mind to play cat and mouse . . . to give me a big come-on until I'm half mad with wanting you, and then snap . . . you pretend to go ice-cold on me? There's a very nasty name for women who get their kicks like that!"

Tears welled up in Tina's eyes, stinging her lids then bursting free and rolling down her cheeks.

"I . . . I'm not like that," she faltered.

"No? So why give me the same capricious treatment, every time—right from that very first kiss, when your car broke down? You sent out all the seductive signals, and when I took you up on them . . . well, you enjoyed yourself for just so long, then suddenly turned on me and tried to make out that I'd taken advantage of you. And every single occasion since then, it's been the same on-off routine." Abruptly he dropped his hold on her wrist, as if feeling contaminated by the very touch of her. "I told you that next time you'd have to come crawling, and by God I meant it! I'm not playing your vile little game any longer."

Tina had been standing there transfixed, half blinded by tears. Now, with a cry that seemed to be wrung from the very depths of her being, she turned and stumbled away from him . . . to the sanctuary of that big luxurious bedroom which should have been his as well. Wrenching open the door, she almost fell inside, slamming it shut behind her and turning the key. A dark mist was enveloping her and she fumbled her way to the bed and threw herself down upon the satin quilt, caught by a paroxysm of weeping which threatened to tear out her very soul. Then, above the sound of her noisy sobbing, she heard a loud rapping on the door.

"Tina!" Brant was shouting. "Let me in!"

"Go away!" she called back wretchedly.

"No," he insisted. "We've got to have this out. Open the door!"

She rose unsteadily and staggered across the room. "Leave me alone, Brant," she begged him through the door panels. "Can't you see, we have nothing to say to each other—not about this."

"We've got some sorting out to do," he responded, and rattled the handle. "So open up at once!"

"Don't make so much noise," she entreated, "or Mrs. Moncrieff will hear."

"I don't care a damn about that," he said in the same thunderous voice. "If you refuse to open this door, Tina, I shall break it down. Now, what's it to be?"

She knew that he wouldn't hesitate to carry out his threat—and their confrontation would be infinitely worse if he'd had to use force to get in. Reluctantly, she unlocked the door and stood back. Brant entered without hurry, closing the door quietly behind him. He advanced on her and Tina shrank back in fear. But he only put his hands on her shoulders and pressed her down into a velvet-covered chair. Then he stood before her, a tall, menacing figure with arms crossed determinedly.

"Straight talking, Tina!" he ordered. "Understand?"

She nodded dumbly.

"Right! I told you once that you're a warm-blooded, sensual woman, and I meant it. No man who'd ever felt you responding as you responded to me would think otherwise about you. So why this stupid business of trying to deny your own nature? Have you got some peculiar grudge against men in general, or is it just *me?*"

The hands lying in her lap kneaded together in agony. She felt trapped, and wanted only to escape.

"Answer my question, Tina!" he rasped implacably.

She somehow found a voice . . . not her own voice! "You only married me because, as heir to Hucclecote Hall, you had to have a wife."

His handsome face darkened. "That's another matter altogether from the one we're discussing now—and something you were perfectly well aware of when you agreed to marry me! Morever, before you even knew who I was, in that first encounter on the road, you behaved in exactly the same blow-hot—blow-cold fashion. One thing you most certainly are not, Tina, is frigid. So, I ask you yet again, what's it all about?"

From somewhere deep in her throat, scarcely audible, came the whisper, "Doesn't it occur to you that it might be myself I hate?"

Hard eyes riveted her. "Explain that!"

"I hate what I am—my own nature." Cornered, Tina had shouted out the words, but now she cowered back into the chair, terrified of what she might have unleashed.

He moved and his hands were on her shoulders again, this time shaking her roughly.

"That's crazy talk, Tina! What the devil do you mean?"

She had been insane to speak so unguardedly. Brant would not be satisfied now until he had extracted the truth from her. And then . . . what triumph for him, to be proved so devastatingly right about the woman he had married with such contempt!

She made a desperate, feeble attempt to evade the inevitable. "I . . . I just meant that I hate myself for ever agreeing to become your wife on the terms I did. It . . . it was dishonest of me. . . ."

"You're lying, Tina! Whatever it was you meant, it's something far more fundamental, far more basic. So out with it!"

She begged weakly. "Let me go, then. I . . . I can't think, when you're being so rough. Please, Brant!"

As if awareness that he was even touching her came only slowly, he withdrew his hands and straightened up. But his gaze still pierced her. And, as always, when he released her from however violent a grasp, Tina felt coldly bereft. She could not remain still under his steel-hard scrutiny. Rising unsteadily to her feet, she stumbled across to the window and rested her head against the cool glass, staring out across the balcony into the darkness of the night. She heard Brant move nearer, and her whole body tensed against his anticipated touch. But he didn't touch her, merely prompting, "Well, tell me!"

"I married you out of spite, Brant," she whispered. "You had revealed to me—*proved* to me—the truth about myself that I'd always dreaded. So I married you to punish myself, and be revenged on you."

"What truth about yourself?" he demanded brusquely.

Why not say it? Why not condemn herself by uttering the damning words, to debase herself as she deserved?

"That . . . that I am my mother all over again," she murmured, her breath coming painfully. "That I'm a woman who is incapable of true love. A woman who spurns the offer of decent love in favour of the cheapest sort of passion."

He spoke quietly, but with an echo of the old scorn. "Whose 'decent' love have you spurned, might I enquire?"

She turned to face him, her eyes glittering with tears. "Charles'."

"But *he* threw you over," Brant objected. "Not you him."

"Because I *drove* him to it, with my shameless behavior." It was almost a relief to apply the whip at last, to scourge herself with suffering. "And you were right, Brant, I *could* have gone after him. I could have pleaded for his forgiveness, begged him to take me back. But I let him go and weakly remained here with you."

Brant's voice was abrasive. "If either of you needed forgiveness, it was that wet fish Medwyn! His conception of love . . ."

"His conception of love," Tina broke in bitterly, "was one of decency and high regard. Of a warm, steady affection."

"You make it sound about as exciting as owning a pet goldfish!" Brant remarked cuttingly. "And you're not far wrong. What was all that about your mother?"

"I told you."

"Details, if you please," he insisted. "So that I can try and sort out what's going on in that muddled brain of yours."

"My mother was unfaithful to my father," she breathed.

"Is that all?" he said scornfully.

"You don't understand," Tina cried. "My father was the most wonderful man . . . utterly devoted to her. But she had a lover! It . . . it turned out later that the affair had lasted a long time, and my father hadn't known because he trusted her absolutely. And

then . . . then one night she was out with this man, and
he crashed his car and they were both killed."

There was silence, then Brant enquired, "When did
this happen? How old were you at the time?"

"I was just three."

Another silence, filled with incredulity. Brant said at
last, "I'm sorry about you losing your mother, of
course. But Heaven's above, all those years ago, and
you're still treating it as high tragedy!"

"You still don't understand!" Tina protested. "Can't
you see . . . what was in my mother's make-up is in
mine, too. I could have had the love of a really fine
man, and I threw it away, just for . . . just for . . ."

Brant's voice was low and ominous. "You threw it
away for what, Tina?"

She felt herself cowering, but somehow she made
herself meet his eyes.

"You've been right about me all along the line,
Brant," she said slowly. "I've been so desperately
afraid, ever since the very first time you kissed me. It
was so casual to you, no more than a joke. But it
unleashed in me what I'd always dreaded, the thing I'd
kept sternly under control." Her eyes, swimmy and
red-rimmed from weeping, looked at him accusingly.
"You took delight in making me respond to you,
despite myself."

"I did!" he agreed. "What normal man wouldn't
delight in getting such a beautiful woman to respond to
him with passion. Not that you've ever really let
yourself go. You'd be quite a volcano if you'd only
throw away those stupid inhibitions of yours."

She felt an almost irresistible impulse to go to him
and strike that sneering face. But she knew the
inevitable outcome. She would be instantly jerked into
those steel-strong arms, held powerless until her resist-

ance melted away. And her husband would have scored yet another of his contemptible victories.

"I hate you, Brant!" she whispered.

"Love-hate?" he turned.

She shook her head, jerkily, like a puppet. "That other word doesn't enter into our relationship, not in the slightest degree."

"Is this your idea of what a marriage *should* be?" he challenged. "A loveless battle?"

"No, yours!" she flashed. "I told you before—as far as you're concerned, I'm merely an insurance policy against disinheritance. Well, I'm ready to keep my side of the bargain, I'll play the role to the best of my ability."

"*In* bed, as well as out?"

"That too, if you require it."

"How big of you!" he mocked. "How unstintingly generous! You propose, I take it, to act like your Victorian great-grandmama might have recommended . . . lie back and think of England! Well, no thanks. I'd prefer to avail myself of a more active bed partner."

"I'm sure you'll have no difficulty," she retorted, "and I wish you joy of her and she of you—until you grow bored and look elsewhere for your sordid pleasures."

His dark eyes glittered with such rage that Tina was afraid he would strike her. Agonising seconds pulsed by, but Brant remained stock still. Then, without another word, he turned on his heel and strode to the door, jerking it open and slamming it behind him with such force that it must certainly have woken Mrs. Moncrieff if she'd managed to sleep through what had gone before. Even the birds nesting in the ivy outside the window were disturbed, and murmured a sleepy protest.

Chapter Fourteen

The pace of life at Hucclecote Hall quickened daily, as preparations for the publicity banquet got under way. It was inevitable, perhaps, that crisis followed upon crisis . . . the caterers made difficulties about the menu, the theatrical costumiers who were to dress the guests in suitable period garb discovered that the date coincided with a festival of Elizabethan drama at a northern town, which meant that their choice of costumes would not be as extensive as normal.

"We'll have to ask people to supply us with their vital statistics before we issue any invitations," Brant observed with a rueful smile. "And we'll only invite the ones who can be suitably rigged out."

It was small consolation for Tina that the working side of their relationship had miraculously survived that disastrous scene in her bedroom. She and Brant were warily polite to one another, and since both were committed to the success of the job in hand, they somehow got by.

The two of them never went riding together now. But Tina so valued the freedom of roaming the estate in the saddle that she made an effort to get out every day, watchful that her ride didn't coincide with Brant's hard gallops on Heracles. She rode Kirsty quietly, seeking out deserted bridle paths where she could be sure of encountering no one, and often she found herself talking to her little mare, confiding her thoughts in a way she could never have done to another human being.

"I despise him utterly, Kirsty," she would whisper. "I loathe and detest his whole attitude to life. And yet I can't help loving him. I love him desperately, with my whole heart and soul. In spite of everything, in spite of his hateful arrogance, his scorn, his taunts and his sneers, I shall love him till the day I die."

An army of women from the village had been engaged to clean and polish the Great Hall·and its surrounding rooms to a state of gleaming perfection. Vast quantities of cutlery and plate were brought out from long-disused pantries to be washed and polished. The girls engaged to act as serving wenches were gigglingly gotten into costume and put through a rehearsal by Tina. There was a long press handout to prepare and get photocopied, and conferences with TV engineers about their lighting requirements, which mustn't be allowed to interfere with the authenticity of the proceedings.

And then, just a day before the great event, when things were at their maddest state of pandemonium, Brant was called to the phone by Mrs. Moncrieff. When he rejoined Tina, he announced that he was going to London.

She stared at him in dismay. "When? How long will you be?"

"Straight away, this minute," he told her. "I may even be staying overnight, I don't know yet."

"But Brant . . . you can't! It's just not fair, with so much left to be done."

"You'll have to cope without me," he said carelessly.

"How can I?" she cried, aghast. "I've got more than enough on my own plate, without taking on what you're scheduled to handle. There's the finalising of the transport to arrange for those coming down by train, and the musicians are coming to test the acoustics, and. . . ."

"All things you can handle perfectly well," he pointed out impatiently.

"Yes, but while I'm doing that, who'll be discussing the flower requirements with the head gardener? And I've got a list of at least a dozen phone calls I've simply got to make."

Brant glanced at his wristwatch. "You'll manage. You're about the most *efficient* beautiful woman I know. Now, I must dash."

Despite the compliment, Tina felt annoyed. "At least you might tell me what it's about," she said bitterly. And when Brant didn't answer, she went on, "Well, whatever it is, can't it wait until after the banquet tomorrow?"

"No," he clipped. "It can't!"

"Why not?" she persisted, really angry now. "What's so vitally important that it has to take precedence over everything else?"

"Questions, questions," he muttered exasperatedly. "You stand there telling me how much there is to be done, and you're simply wasting time! I'll see you when I see you."

He was gone. A few minutes later, from a window of the Great Hall, Tina watched the white Mercedes sweeping off down the long curving driveway.

A small, sharp-faced man was at her elbow.

"Mrs. Wakefield, could I have a word, please?" He turned out to be a reporter from the local weekly paper, which was due to go to press before the banquet, and he was asking for some advance information. It was half an hour before Tina had satisfied him and could get away upstairs and seek out Mrs. Moncrieff.

First she asked the housekeeper an unnecessary question about her own well-organised side of the arrangements for tomorrow. Then, trying to sound casual, she added, "By the way, who was that on the phone to my husband?"

Mrs. Moncrieff frowned, looking puzzled. "Oh, you mean a wee while back?" she said. "Let me see now, I'm not sure that I can remember her name."

"*Her* name?"

Tina was awarded a frankly curious glance, and felt herself blushing. She was aware—it had been obvious the next morning—that the housekeeper must have overheard her and Brant quarrelling on the night of the dinner party. Perhaps, therefore, Mrs. Moncrieff had now leapt to the same ugly suspicion as Tina herself, for a guarded look came into her long, thin face.

"Oh, did I say *her?*" she enquired, with heavy innocence.

Tina met the housekeeper's eyes squarely, because she *had* to know. "Yes, you did, Mrs. Moncrieff," she confirmed. "What was her name, if you please?"

"Oh, er . . . let me see now. It was Gray, I think. Yes, that's right . . . Mrs. Nicola Gray. I believe," she added uncomfortably, "that it was something to do with the arrangements for tomorrow evening, Mrs. Wakefield."

"Oh?" Tina's heart quickened with hope. "Did she say so?"

"Well no, not exactly."

"What *did* she say, then?"

Unable to meet Tina's challenging eyes any longer, the housekeeper's gaze slid away. "Nothing, really," she mumbled. "She just asked if Mr. Wakefield was at home and could she speak to him please. I explained that the master was very busy, but she said it was extremely important and that she knew he'd want to

speak to her." Suddenly Mrs. Moncrieff looked at Tina
again and spoke urgently, woman to woman. "He's a
fine man, lassie, you must believe that's true. If you'll
just give it time, everything will come right for you. I'm
as certain of that as. . . ."

She saw the pain in Tina's eyes and faltered to a halt.
Then, pleadingly, she began again. "Men see this sort
of thing differently from we women, you know. It's a
fact of life we just have to learn to live with."

"I've tried to," Tina said wretchedly, and put her
hands to her face trying to hold back tears.

"Look, lovey," said the housekeeper sympathetical-
ly, "why don't you take ten minutes off and let me
make you a nice cup of tea?"

Tina shook her head and smiled bravely. She had
managed to pull herself together now. "No thanks,
Mrs. Moncrieff," she said with dignity, as if the
momentary lapse had never happened. "There's so
much to be done, and I really must get on."

Tina forced her mind to concentrate on the long list
of jobs on hand, ticking them off one by one as they
were completed. By evening, when the last of the
various workmen and other outsiders had left the house
to its usual slumbrous quiet, she felt unutterably weary.
But she could not rest, every nerve in her body was at
screaming point.

The phone rang several times, but it was never
Brant. She had to give her attention to some small
query raised by the person at the other end of the line,
when all she wanted was to slam the phone back in its
cradle and wait tensely for it to ring again, in the hope
that it might be him next time.

Eventually she went to bed. But not to sleep. Her
thoughts were all with her husband . . . and that
woman he was with. It was one of the worst nights she
could ever remember.

The morning of the banquet was one of shimmering autumnal beauty. Tina lingered for a few moments at the window of her lonely bedroom, gazing out across the park and listening to the sweet medley of birdsong. The crescent lake glittered, silver-gilt in the sunlight, and upon its knoll the little Grecian temple gleamed whitely.

A phrase slipped unbidden into her mind. "This is my day of destiny." She shivered and turned away from the morning's beauty, dressing quickly in readiness to face the first arrivals, who would be here by eight o'clock . . . the women who were to arrange the great troughs of flowers fetched in by the gardeners, a display as lavish as the banks of roses on her wedding day.

The whole morning was one long rush, the Great Hall milling with people all constantly turning to Tina for decisions. And still no word from Brant! She managed, under Mrs. Moncrieff's coaxing, to eat an omelette for her lunch, though every mouthful was an effort. Then a van arrived bringing the costumes, all packed and labelled for the individual guests, and these had to be distributed to various bedrooms earmarked as changing rooms. There were caterer's men everywhere, dashing between kitchens and the Great Hall, cannoning into each other, shouting almost loudly enough to drown out the quartet of fiddlers in the Minstrels' Gallery who were trying to rehearse *Greensleeves*.

A dreadful fear descended upon Tina, growing almost to certainty, that Brant wasn't going to come at all. Because of that woman, he had abandoned her to cope alone tonight. How could she manage without him? The whole banquet would be a fiasco, without rhyme or reason. He was the king-pin upon which everything else depended.

And then, when she had virtually given up all hope, he was there. Not striding in through the main entrance door, but descending the stairs as if from their private apartment. As he came towards her, the expression on his face was unreadable.

"Oh Brant," she gasped, on a wave of thankfulness. "I thought you were never coming! I thought . . . I thought. . . ." And then the final threads of self-control to which she'd been clinging so desperately seemed to snap, and she burst into a storm of weeping.

Blinded by tears, she felt her husband's arms supporting her, drawing her away from all the bustle. He led her into the small sitting room, the one in which he had first interviewed her the day she had arrived at Hucclecote Hall.

Brant's voice was surprisingly gentle as he asked, "What did you mean out there just now about thinking I was never coming? What exactly *was* it you thought?"

She drew in a deep, shuddering breath. "I thought . . . I thought you weren't going to bother coming back tonight because you were too occupied with that woman. Mrs. Nicola Gray," she added, nearly spitting it out.

Brant stared at her in astonishment. "You know her name? But how is that possible?"

"Mrs. Moncrieff," she murmured.

His dark eyes narrowed in swift anger. "She ran to you telling tales?"

"No, it wasn't like that," Tina felt obliged to explain. "I *made* her tell me. I forced her to say who it was who had phoned you."

"I see! And you've been thinking. . . ." He paused, then said, "I want you to meet her, Tina."

She started violently. "Meet her! But you can't mean that, Brant . . . it's cruel of you."

"No, it's not cruel," he denied. "I've brought her back with me specially. She's upstairs in the apartment, waiting."

Every instinct in Tina's body rebelled at the thought. "I won't see her," she protested wildly. "I won't, I won't. Why should I?"

"Because it's important," he said implacably. "Nicola Gray is the one person you should have met years ago."

"*Years ago* . . . but I don't understand." She stared up at him in utter bewilderment. "Brant, who *is* this woman?"

"Gray is her married name," he told her. "Before that she was Nicola Whiting."

Tina's brain was too clogged with the wretchedness of these past hours, with the outrage of what Brant seemed to be demanding of her now, to register the name with any comprehension.

"Am I . . . am I supposed to know her?" she whispered.

"You should," he replied grimly. "It's taken me some time to track her down. . . . there wasn't a lot to go on, even for one of the best enquiry agents in the country. But Nicola Whiting used to have a brother, Tina, and his name was Graham. Now do you know who she is?"

Tremors of shock shuddered through her. "Graham Whiting? You . . . you mean . . .?"

"Yes, I do. The man who was your mother's lover."

Against her will, Tina found herself being led upstairs by Brant to their private apartment. As they entered the drawing room a woman rose from a chair by the marble fireplace. She was around fifty, Tina judged, but well preserved, with a slender figure and good complexion. She wore an elegant summer suit in cream linen, with tan accessories.

Brant made the introductions. "This is my wife," he said. "Tina, this is Mrs. Nicola Gray. And now I'll leave you to talk."

"No Brant, you mustn't go," Tina protested in dismay, as he turned towards the door.

"Yes," he said gently. "It's better this way."

Nicola Gray stepped forward impulsively. "Please, Mrs. Wakefield . . . I'm sure your husband is right. It would be better for us to talk alone."

"Very well," Tina murmured reluctantly.

When Brant had left them, she remembered her manners and invited her guest to sit down again. Taking the armchair opposite, she began stiffly, "Now, Mrs. Gray, what is it you have to tell me? I understand it is something to do with my mother . . . and your brother."

"That is so. Your husband thinks—and I agree with him—that there are facts about their relationship which should be made known to you."

"I think I know quite enough already," Tina replied with cold dignity. "I know that, when they met their death together, they were engaged in a sordid intrigue."

A cloud crossed Nicola Gray's face. "You sound very bitter, my dear. Can't you try, instead, to think of them as two people who were desperately in love?"

"How could they be?" Tina demanded. "There was only one man my mother had any right to love . . . her husband. The man she had vowed to love till death did them part, and who loved her in return. Yet she cheated my father in the worst way a woman can possibly cheat her husband."

In her agitation Tina jumped to her feet, and went

nervously to the window. She was aware, as she stood there blindly looking out, that Nicola Gray had also risen, and now came to stand beside her.

"Your father was a very fine man," she said after a moment. "In his way, he was devoted to your mother . . . but whether such devotion can be called love, as most people understand the word, is open to doubt. The thing that was all important to your father, Mrs. Wakefield, was his work at the University."

"Was that so wrong of him?" Tina cried passionately, hardly thinking what she was saying.

"Not wrong, perhaps. But neither is it easy for a woman to find herself taking a minor role in her husband's life."

All Tina's instincts, all her filial loyalty, made her want to refute what Mrs. Gray was trying to tell her . . . that her father had not been entirely perfect, her mother not entirely to blame for her infidelity. And yet, weakening her will to protest, came the wistful memories of long ago . . . a sweet, gentle-faced woman bending over her cot, crooning her softly to sleep.

"You seem to know a lot about it all, Mrs. Gray," she said rebelliously.

The older woman nodded. "Yes, I do. As it happens I was very much in the picture." She reached out impulsively and touched Tina's hand. "It's a long story, my dear. May I tell it to you?"

Tina hesitated, then nodded her assent. When they were seated again, on a scrolled sofa near the window, Nicola Gray began to speak in her evenly-modulated voice.

"When I first met your mother, she was younger than you are now," she said. "Not yet twenty, in fact. She was a lovely girl, very much like you to look at. Graham used to bring her round to our house quite often—I'm a widow now, but my husband and I lived in a town not far from Bellchester at that time. My brother and I were very close, having lost both our parents when we were still in our early teens. Not that Graham needed to confide in me that he and Deidre were head over heels in love. I've rarely seen two people as ecstatically happy as those two were all through that summer."

"And what . . . what went wrong?" Tina whispered.

Mrs. Gray made a helpless little gesture with her hands. "Perhaps they were too young . . . Graham was only just over twenty himself. Perhaps they fell too deeply in love too quickly, I don't know. But suddenly there was the most dreadful quarrel. I was never able to get to the bottom of it, but Graham came to me in a state of utter desperation and said he wanted to go abroad—anywhere, so long as it was far away from England. I tried to talk him out of it, but it was no use. I even went to see Deidre, and I met with the same flat refusal to listen to reason. It was heartbreaking to see what they were doing to one another, and all over something quite trivial as far as I could make out. And then Graham's firm suddenly agreed to transfer him to their office in Montreal, and off he went. I tried to keep in touch with Deidre, because I couldn't believe it was really all over between her and Graham, but she moved away and I heard she'd taken a secretarial job at the University in Bellchester. I could hardly believe the next news I had of her, only about three months later. It was that she had married a brilliant young professor there.

"I hated having to tell Graham this," Nicola went on, "but I thought it was for the best—so he wouldn't go on hoping for a reconciliation. Then, as time went by, I began to think that he'd finally gotten over Deidre, because he mentioned various girlfriends and it looked as if something might come of one or two of them. But it never did. And after nearly five years he was transferred back to this country. I shall never forget the evening—he'd been home about a month—that Graham came round to see me. He looked, I don't really know how to describe it . . . deeply shocked, and yet somehow elated at the same time. 'I've seen her, Nicky,' he told me. I asked him who he meant, although of course I knew already. 'I've seen Deidre,' he said. 'I ran into her by chance in Bellchester this afternoon. And Nicky, she's not happily married at all. Anybody can see that. She's just as miserable as I am.'"

"You . . . you should have put a stop to it," Tina protested shakily. "You should have prevented your brother from seeing any more of her."

Nicola Gray gave an unhappy sigh. "Do you think I didn't try? But nothing I could say made any difference. He kept saying, 'I can't go on living without her, Nicky! I've never stopped cursing myself for that stupid quarrel we had.'"

"What happened?" Tina asked. She was trembling all over.

"During those next few weeks they met several times. And afterwards, Graham would either be on top of the world because he thought he stood a chance with Deidre, or sunk in a terrible depression. The poor girl was obviously torn in two, unable to make up her mind. I dared not interfere, but then one day Deidre phoned me and asked if we could meet."

She fell silent, as if lost in her memories. From the Great Hall, Tina could hear the distant sounds of preparations for the banquet, but somehow it all seemed utterly remote and unreal now.

"It was a lovely autumn day like this," Nicola Gray continued at length. "I picked Deidre up near the

University and we drove to a quiet spot where we could talk in peace. And there she opened up her heart to me. She told me how desperately she was in love with my brother. How she had loved him all along, in a way that she had never been able to love her husband. Graham was begging her to leave Ernest Harcourt and go to him, taking you with her, of course. And Deidre confessed to me that the thought of this was unbearably sweet to her. And yet . . . Ernest had shown her nothing but kindness in his rather absent-minded way. It was just that he was an unemotional sort of man, and it wasn't his fault that he never lit in her the sort of flame that Graham could, merely by a look, merely by the touch of his hand."

Tina felt a little shiver run through her body. Merely a look, merely the touch of a hand . . . it was by just so little that Brant could ignite that tormenting flame within *her*. Like mother, like daughter. . . .

"That's all very well," she stammered huskily. "But whatever loyalty she felt for my father didn't stop her going on deceiving him, being unfaithful. . . ."

Nicola Gray's brown eyes were turned upon her in puzzlement. "What makes you so certain that she *was* unfaithful?"

"My aunt . . . Aunt Ruth," Tina explained. "She was very bitter about it."

"Ah yes, your father's sister! Deidre spoke of her to me. A good woman, doubtless . . . but a woman of narrow views. It seems that she had always regarded Deidre with the deepest suspicion, from the day her brother announced his engagement to her." She glanced at Tina with compassion. "It's obvious that she went out of her way to poison your mind against Deidre."

"No, that's not fair!" Tina protested. "Aunt Ruth devoted her life to bringing me up after my mother was killed. She only told me what she did to . . . to warn me. . . ."

There was no need for her to elaborate. Nicola said quietly, "To warn you against something of which she hadn't the faintest glimmer of understanding! Your mother, my dear, was the very opposite of her sister-in-law . . . she was a warm and generous-hearted woman, with the ability to love deeply and passionately."

"Love?" Tina queried in a whisper.

"What else?" A tiny frown creased Nicola's smooth forehead. Then she went on gently, "I think I understand why your husband wanted you to hear what I could tell you. Let me assure you of this, my dear Tina—from one who was blissfully happy for many years until I lost my husband. The gift your mother bestowed upon you is one of the most precious gifts in the world . . . a blessing to be cherished, not a curse."

Tina began to shake her head in vehement protest, but before she could speak the older woman put out a hand to check her.

"Please let me finish my story," she said firmly, "so that you will know the truth about your mother—the real truth, not some distorted half-truth. That day we met, Deidre told me that her decision was finally made. She had agreed to meet my brother that same evening, and she would tell him they must say goodbye and never meet again, because her loyalty was owed to her husband and the child she had borne him. She wanted to tell me, she said, because she wanted me to help Graham through the sorrow and desolation she knew he would be facing . . . she did not speak of the suffering she herself would have to endure. When we said goodbye, Deidre clung to me, sobbing, and I thought her heart would break."

"And . . . and that same evening, they were killed?" Tina asked in a hoarse whisper.

Nicola bent her head in sad acknowledgement. "I waited up late, expecting that Graham would phone or call round to see me . . . just to unburden himself, you know. Instead, it was the police who came, to break the terrible news. There was a lorry involved, too, with faulty brakes. Graham was a good driver, but perhaps in his misery he wasn't taking his usual care. At any rate, in avoiding the lorry his car ran off the road and they were both killed instantly."

Tears were pouring down Tina's cheeks now, but she made no move to stem them, while her hands twisted and untwisted with horror and pity.

Nicola Gray said gently, "Your mother's great capacity for loving won't have died, my dear Tina, as long as it lives on in you. She would rest content, I feel sure, if she could know that her daughter hadn't made the tragic mistake of marrying the wrong kind of man."

"But I have, I have!" Tina burst out wretchedly. "Oh, not in the same way . . . for entirely different reasons. But I too am married to a man who isn't capable of true love."

The older woman's eyes opened in amazement. "You cannot really believe that!" she reproached Tina.

"I do! He has virtually told me so himself. He scorns the very idea of love between a man and a woman."

Was it an exclamation of impatience from Nicola Gray? "If you demand that a man should humble himself before you, baring his heart, you will have to wait a long time, my dear. A man—a normal man—will have desired many women before he meets the right one. And when he does, when he suspects that he feels something altogether different for her than he felt for all those who went before . . . can you expect him to rush to admit it, even to himself? But let that woman show that *she* loves *him,* then he will very soon find all the right words to express his emotions."

Tina quenched the flame of hope that was leaping in her, and said obstinately, "Brant doesn't love me."

"No?" Nicola Gray queried. "Why then did he move heaven and earth to trace someone who had known your mother and the man she loved . . . someone close to them both?" She smiled gently at Tina. "In the end your husband tracked me down in Jersey, which is my home now. He wrote and asked what information I could give him concerning the circumstances in which your mother and my brother met their death. And when I replied, he wrote again begging me to meet you, to let him bring you to Jersey, because he thought it important for you to hear the story from my own lips. But as it happened, I was already planning to come this way to visit relatives. So I decided to bring the date forward, and here I am."

Tina flushed with shame. "When Brant rushed off to London after a Mrs. Nicola Gray had telephoned him, and stayed away all night, I thought . . ." She broke off, too embarrassed to continue.

"I telephoned to say that I'd be arriving in London last night, but then a freak storm over the Channel Islands grounded the plane, and I didn't arrive until today," Nicola explained. She gave a soft laugh. "So you were eaten up with jealousy, were you? Look into your heart, my dear Tina, and then try to deny to me that you are deeply in love with your husband."

Chapter Fifteen

Time had passed more quickly than either of the two women had realised. Nicola Gray delayed only long enough for a cup of tea before hurrying off to catch a train back to London. Tina pressed her to stay for the banquet, but Nicola explained that she had arranged to go to the theatre that evening with her friends.

"Thank you so very much for coming," Tina said, the simple words spoken straight from her heart.

"It's been good for me, too, my dear," Nicola affirmed. "Perhaps I have done for you what, sadly, I couldn't do for my brother and your mother . . . smoothed the path of love a little."

"Let's keep in touch," Tina suggested impulsively.

"Yes, I should like that," the older woman agreed, and they embraced with genuine affection.

Fifteen minutes later, Mrs. Moncrieff found Tina daydreaming in her bedroom.

"This won't do, Mrs. Wakefield," she admonished. "It's high time for you to be getting into your costume."

Still too dazed to think clearly, Tina accepted the housekeeper's help in getting dressed.

"Where is my husband?" she asked.

"He'll be changing too, I hope! I warned him that time was slipping by."

Tina was alone again, sitting before her dressing-table mirror, adjusting the little heart-shaped cap trimmed with pearls, when Brant came to her. The sight of him made her catch her breath. He looked so achingly handsome in a crimson doublet and hose, his fur-trimmed cloak slung dashingly across one shoulder. She rose to meet him, moving slowly in the unaccustomed farthingale.

Brant stopped in his tracks, his eyes brilliant with admiration. He swept off his plumed hat and bowed low in obeisant homage.

"You are beautiful, my lady wife," he breathed softly.

Tina was about to brush aside his compliment with a deprecating little laugh. But she changed her mind.

"You look rather splendid yourself, husband of mine. A born and bred Elizabethan gentleman-adventurer!"

Their eyes, searching into each other's, were saying so much more than any words could do. From somewhere in the house she heard a clock chime, and it reminded her of the inexorable passage of time.

"Brant, we must go downstairs. . . ." she stammered, feeling her skin growing warm under the intensity of his gaze.

"Not yet!" he said quickly, coming to her and gripping her shoulders with fingers that were gentle yet possessive. "You talked to Nicola Gray, then?"

Tina nodded her head. "Oh Brant, I've been such a fool," she whispered. "Can you ever forgive me?"

He put his finger against her lips to silence her. "It's I who have been a fool," he corrected. "A fool not to have shown more understanding, not to tell you what I really thought about you . . . how much I love you."

"Do you really love me?" she asked tremblingly.

"You'll never know how deeply, my darling Tina.

You have insidiously twined yourself around my senses until you are part of my very being, and I cannot imagine life without you." His eyes lingered lovingly on her face. "That first moment we met I knew that I wanted you, needed you . . . a feeling I tried to dismiss as a familiar masculine desire, easily assuaged, if not with you then with some other girl. But as day followed day that need for you became obsessive. You tormented my thoughts, both waking and sleeping. I had never before known such an intensity of desire, yet always you turned away from me with contempt in your eyes."

"The contempt was for myself, Brant! Because you could so easily arouse in me those dark forces that terrified me."

"Dark forces?"

"That was how I thought of them—at the time."

"And now?"

"I am beginning to understand myself better," she murmured shyly. "But Brant, we *must* go downstairs."

"Damn you, Tina!" he said on a quick catch of breath. "Always it's the same with you . . . you come so far to meet me, then you hastily retreat—as if you find a twisted pleasure in putting me on the rack." His voice shook with underlying passion. "Don't you understand what risks you run, tormenting me like this? There have been times when I could have killed you, crushed you to death with these two hands of mine."

She shivered, afraid of his passion yet exulting in it. "But Brant, I have never refused you—not once since we've been married.

"And do you imagine that meagre offering sufficed?" he demanded, with an echo of his old bitterness. "I've had greater generosity than that from many other women, women who have given themselves to me for the sheer delight of the moment. And that was enough for me . . . from them. From you, I thought at first that it would be enough to have just the mere possession of your body. But what I craved for beyond everything was your *love*." Brant raked long fingers through his dark hair. "I was fighting against my instincts at the time, trying to convince myself that marrying Loretta Boyd-French was a sane and sensible business arrangement, with her seductive body thrown in as a bonus. But I've come to realise that if Loretta hadn't rejected me when she did, I would have been the one to make the break. In those early days, Tina, I cursed the blue-eyed girl who had come between Loretta and myself in my thoughts, the girl who made Loretta's sophistication seem shallow and trivial beyond bearing. Cursed her, yet at the same time burned with love for her. You, my darling Tina, seemed to hold out a tantalising vision of heaven to me. Yet you kept despatching me to hell."

"I wanted to," she confessed frankly. "I wanted to make you suffer."

"And you succeeded beyond your wildest dreams! Did you hate me so very much?"

"Yes," she whispered. "I hated you for what you were doing to me. For making me love you."

"And do you love me still?"

Tina nodded her head in quick affirmation, the depth of her feeling for him shining in her eyes. With rough tenderness Brant gathered her into his arms.

"Never look at another man, my darling one," he threatened, "for I shall hate him violently and be his enemy for life."

"And I shall hate any other woman you look at," Tina murmured into his shoulder.

A joyful laugh came from deep in Brant's throat. "You have no need to worry, beloved, for I shall only ever have eyes for you. My darling, beautiful wife! I warn you, all the years ahead of us will not be long enough to assuage the hunger I feel for you."

His lips came down on hers in a long, passionate kiss that sent a great warm joy flooding through her. She felt Brant's body quicken against hers in throbbing urgency and then his hands were roaming over her, moulding themselves to her soft curves. Exultantly, Tina pressed herself closer against him, feeling weak and dizzy with love for him. Her own hunger had been awakened now and threatened to sweep her towards a wild oblivion. But a shred of sanity remained. As he began to thrust her back towards the bed, she managed to gasp, "No Brant . . . not now! Our guests will be assembling, and we must go down to welcome them."

He shut his ears to her protests and urged softly against her hair, "Come, let me take off these obstructing garments of yours. I want to see you again in your naked perfection. I want to love you, my darling, and have you love me. Now at last we shall really find each other."

With the strength of her new-born confidence Tina pushed herself away from him.

"We have *already* found each other, Brant darling," she said firmly yet tenderly. "Is it too much to give up a single evening to our guests? They have been invited here, and we cannot fail them."

"A whole evening!" he sighed. "Long hours to be wasted in eating and drinking and idle conversation when I only want to be with you—loving you, possessing you, consuming you. . . ."

Did he imagine it was any easier for her? The tormenting flame was raging through her veins, flaring to new heights of desire now that shame no longer damped it down. How was she going to tear herself

away from the arms of her husband, her lover, for an
evening of Elizabethan merrymaking?

She murmured softly, her voice husky with love,
"The evening will pass, Brant darling, and afterwards
. . . afterwards there will be the night."

He smiled, in rueful resignation to the call of duty.

"And after tonight, ten thousand nights to come!" he
said. "I warn you, my darling, lovely wife, that I shall
never grow tired of you, of passionately loving you. I
shall know this sweet torment of wanting you all the
days of my life."

Somehow, the simple words that had never before
passed Tina's lips came so easily now. "I love you,
Brant."

"And always will?" he demanded.

"Always and forever!" she vowed. "Now, kiss me
once more and then we must go downstairs."

How naive of her not to realise that another kiss
would threaten to steal away her last fragments of
willpower. Her lips parted eagerly before his and she
felt the warm sweet singing of her senses. Despite the
unfamiliar clothes they wore, their bodies seemed to
find each other with aching familiarity, soft curve to
hard muscle. Tina shuddered in ecstasy at the throbbing beat of his desire, and in those wild moments of
mounting passion she herself could so easily have
begged him to throw duty and discretion to the
winds. . . .

A sharp tap on the door brought them both to
sudden awareness. Mrs. Moncrieff called anxiously,
"Mrs. Wakefield . . . it's getting terribly late. People
are waiting for you."

"Just coming!" It was Brant who answered in a
shaken voice—perhaps surprising the housekeeper by
his presence in his wife's bedroom. With a sigh, he

allowed his arms to fall away from their tig
but his eyes held Tina's in the wrench of parting.

"Damn the banquet!" he muttered. "Damn the
estate, and everything else that demands our attention.
Why can't we fly away together to some idyllic desert
island where we can be entirely alone?"

"We'll be on our desert island tonight, Brant," she
promised.

"I adore you, my darling Tina," he breathed huskily,
and raised her hand to press his lips to it before finally
letting her go. "And every single time you catch my eye
this evening, that's what I'll be saying to you, over and
over again."

Tina's arm resting on Brant's, the two of them
paused at the last turn of the wide oak staircase, and
smiled down at their guests. A ripple of comment ran
through the assembled company, and those in the
Great Hall crowded nearer to the archway to see their
host and hostess.

They made a superbly handsome couple, everyone agreed. He so ruggedly and swashbucklingly
handsome—a figure straight out of the first Elizabethan
age—his wife so dazzlingly lovely in her magnificent
gown of dark blue velvet, the loops of pearls across her
bosom gleaming white against the becoming pink of her
satiny skin . . . her heightened colouring explained
away by the warm evening and the excitement of this
splendid occasion.

There was a spontaneous burst of applause and Brant
bowed to his guests, while Tina sketched a deep
curtsey. She could see, among the many faces gathered
below them, Jeff Lintott and Gillian Rowley, standing
together, looking very happy this evening. And there
was something else—something in Jeff's quick reaction

na that her wondrous new-
rant was transparent to him.
ps, for all the world to see.
essed hers in a reassuring message
, their heads held high they proudly
last flight of stairs. The Master of
all and his Lady.

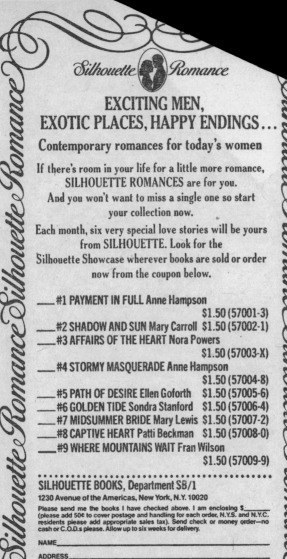